A Pocketful of Pyskies
A Buttonwood Bay Mystery
Piper Dow

Chapter 1

Tia Jenkins backed down the driveway toward the street, letting her foot just ease off the brake and allowing the driveway's incline to dictate the van's speed before coming to a full stop at the edge of the neighbor's shrubs. She grimaced and craned backward in the seat, attempting to see through the overgrown hedge, even though she knew it was futile.

It was difficult in the winter, when there were no leaves on the trees, never mind now that the lilacs were in full bloom. With a little growl of frustration she eased off the brake again, hoping her slow roll into the street would give enough notice to any motorists taking their side road that she was on her way.

The van was fully out of the driveway when Tia's attention caught on a pair of furiously whirring wings hovering at the edge of the lilac nearest the street. A pyskie, but it looked like he was caught on something. Tia pulled the van against the curb and hopped out. The pyskie squealed in panic as she approached and tugged harder on his foot, revealing a shimmering, almost translucent thread wrapped around his ankle.

"Stay away!" The pyskie's command was shrill, an attempt at bravado that Tia blithely ignored.

"I'm not going to hurt you," she breathed, trying to calm the frantic creature. She scanned the ground for an appropriately sized twig to use, while musing, "who would put a magical trapline here?"

Frowning, she picked up a broken branch and used the end to hook the iridescent line. The thread recoiled with a faint ping, sending the pyskie somersaulting backward from the force of his tugging. He recovered and zipped upward in a glittery blur, sounding a small squeak of surprise at his sudden freedom. Tia laughed softly at his maneuvers. Plenty of people treated the sprites like vermin, but she had always found their behavior amusing.

Tia climbed back into the van as her phone sounded over the van's bluetooth connection. She pulled away from the curb before hitting the button to accept the call. "Hey, Cookie! How's it going?"

Ginger Williams's exaggerated groan filled the vehicle and Tia winced. She spun the volume knob quickly before offering sympathy for her best friend's plight.

"Oh no, what's going on?"

"It's those urchins again! I've got to wonder what their mums are thinking." A noise like skin slapping skin sounded, and Tia knew Cookie had just whacked herself with a palm on the forehead. It was a trademark Cookie move. "Oh my gosh, that's the problem, right there! They're bloody well NOT thinking! And I can't smack the little maggots, or hit 'em with a saucepan, or there goes my shop!" She grumbled again, before adding, "'course, if they ruin all the books, there goes my shop, too."

The van filled with a slurping sound as Cookie took a sip of her coffee. Tia heard the protest of creaking springs and knew Cookie was taking a break in the back room, probably leaning back in the old office chair behind a closed door. Tia's lips twitched as she pictured Cookie chasing the neighborhood children through the cafe with a spatula or saucepan, but before she could offer encouragement, Cookie continued.

"Seriously, Tia, it's like their mums are afraid to bring 'em home until dinner." She added in an undertone, "Well, they probably are, if they treat their own homes the way they treat my cafe!" Redirecting her comments to Tia, she sighed. "I've thought of posting signs announcing that unsupervised children will be gifted with an espresso and a free kitten, but I don't think that would faze them. What else can I do? I don't want to scare off the customers. On the other hand, I can't sell damaged products, and I found two pages torn out of one of the picture books this morning."

Tia flicked the directional to take the on-ramp for the highway. She pictured the cozy sitting room at The Gingersnap, with the armchairs and side tables tucked into nooks near the bookshelves lining the room, while a few sets of tables and chairs occupied the center of the space.

"Where are the mothers, and where are the kids when this is happening?" Tia struggled to imagine how the children could be destroying Cookie's merchandise in front of their parents, but there wasn't anywhere obvious for them to hide while being destructive.

Another exasperated huff. "They're all right there! They're just chatting among themselves and not watching their little rugrats. It'd almost be better if they had left the kids behind while they went for a walk or something. This way it feels like they watched the kids destroy my products and then hid the evidence!" Another murmured comment slipped through the phone, "Not sure if the fact they didn't hide it well is more insulting or not. Like, did they think they didn't have to because I'm too stupid to find it? Or too much of a pushover to do anything about it?" Her voice returned to full volume again. "Anyway, that's my problem. What's your day looking like?"

Tia explained that she'd been corralled to run her mother's errands in preparation for the town's Spring Fling in a week and a half. "I don't mind helping her, you know I don't. I just wish she didn't have so many things requiring me to drop what I'm doing to go do whatever it is right away. I had just gotten started on a project when she asked me to grab tablecloths at Penney's, but the list she handed me has a lot more than that on it." Tia shook her head in bemusement as she pulled into the parking lot. "I was in Providence for six years and she managed without me here as errand girl. I've been back in Buttonwood Bay for six months and we're back into the same old routines."

"She only sends you on errands because you agree to go." Cookie's words were muffled around whatever she was eating. "I mean, what would she do if you said no?"

Tia's chest filled with something heavy, but she pushed it, and Cookie's question, away. "Oh, I don't know, probably sublet my room to more Nowbies. Hey, look, I'm at Penney's. I'm going to go in and see what they've got for her tablecloths. I'll see how long this list takes, maybe I can swing by this afternoon."

Agreeing to the tentative plan, they hung up. Tia took a deep breath, closing her eyes and settling her thoughts before climbing out of the van. *Right. Tablecloths.*

***

The clerk at Penney's called three other stores before finding one that had the rest of the tablecloths Tia needed. Luckily, that store was across the parking lot from a Walmart, so she was able to knock off a portion of the list quickly. It was still well after noon before she returned to Buttonwood Bay.

Cookie's cafe, The Gingersnap, sat at one end of the town's Main Street, the opposite end of the town's center from Merserves' Bakery. The center was only a few blocks long, with brick storefronts lining the wide sidewalks. The waterfront was two blocks away; Main Street ran parallel to the shoreline. The town hall boasted a large front lawn that was often used for events, and Buttonwood trees with their camouflage-patterned trunks lined the main streets. It was a nice walk, and a lovely day, and Tia had been stuck in the car for too long. She swung the van into a spot in the town's parking lot and hopped out.

She headed to Merserves for the last few items on her mother's list; a sampling of pastries for dessert, and chocolate croissants for breakfast. Tia's mother had started Jenkins' Events a few months after Tia moved to Providence. Now, six years later, the business was flourishing. Recently, one of the bakeries she normally used had gone out of business, so she was sampling additional wares from other shops to adjust her list of vendors. The Gingersnap was already on her list, of course, but Cookie didn't bake everything Tia's mother needed, and she liked to highlight different items from various bakeries in the area to help drive the local economy. She already served Merserves' croissants, but wanted to give their other dainties another whirl.

Selecting a few of the flaky pastries from the case for tomorrow's breakfast, Tia added them to her mother's order and went back out to the sidewalk. She thought about putting the goodies in the van before stopping in at The Gingersnap to avoid the awkwardness of displaying the bakery's packaging in the cafe, but the warmth of the day would be amplified in the vehicle, and she wasn't sure how the fillings would handle the heat. Instead, she dug a tiny bundle from her purse and unrolled it to reveal a reusable shopping bag large enough to slide the Merserves bag of purchases into. Smiling at the clever hack to disguise her purchases, she strolled through town to Cookie's.

"Good afternoon," she called brightly to Zinnia Rosewood, the Kromera woman who ran the flower shop.

The woman murmured an absent greeting in return before lifting her face from the sandwich board sign she was organizing and recognizing Tia. Her smile brightened and her green hair almost glowed. "Good afternoon! I have some thick cardboard boxes that held a shipment that came in yesterday; I saved them for you. Will you be collecting today?"

Tia pursed her lips as she tried to think of anything else on her schedule. "I can come back and get them this evening. If I can't get here before you close, could you leave them in the back? Thank you so much for thinking of me!"

"Of course, Tia! I'm so happy to help you keep materials out of the landfills. I just wish more people would have your conscience." She tucked her hair behind a pointed ear and bent again to finish her sign.

Tia bent to give Zinnia's potted hearthchime roses a sniff, smiling as the blossoms swayed and tinkled at her nearness. "I can't believe the way you get these things to grow. My mom has some near the back patio, but hers are never this active!"

Zinnia glanced over at the large pot with gentle fondness, the hue of her green hair somehow brightening before she returned her attention to her lettering. "They're doing well on the sidewalk; they love the attention they get! If your back patio doesn't get used much, your mother's might be lonely. I'd suggest moving them to the dooryard that sees the most traffic, they'll be happier. Happy plants are healthier plants!"

Tia raised her eyebrows in surprise, then nodded. "I bet you're right! I'll tell her. Thanks! And, I'll stop by tonight for the boxes." She hummed a little as she continued toward Cookie's. It felt right, today, that she had returned home and was helping her community to be a little brighter spot on the map.

Bold letters sprawling across the wide plate-glass windows advertised her destination: The Gingersnap; Baked Bites for

Bookworms. A tiny bell jingled as she pulled the door open. Tia inhaled the heady aroma of warm cinnamon, vanilla, and brown sugar. Her stomach reminded her instantly that she'd kept lunch light specifically so she could indulge while she visited Cookie.

"Tia! You're just in time, Luv!" Cookie's copper waves were corralled by her chef's ball cap, escaping through the hole in the back to trail down past her shoulders. She ducked back down behind the counter and continued adding coconut macaroons to the tray in the display case. "I've got some fresh oatmeal raisin cookies on the cooling rack! I have coffee shortbread, chocolate chip bars, or these macaroons, too. You'll want the oatmeal, though, so come through to the back." She grinned as she stood, dusting her hands off and motioning to the door of the kitchen. When Tia grinned back and nodded, Cookie turned to Nikola Chuffey, the barista working the counter, to let her know they'd be a few minutes.

Nikola nodded and took a dishpan to bus the coffee cups and plates that had been left on the counter in front of the window. "I've got it," she assured Cookie.

Cookie bustled across to the cookies cooling on the rack and slid one onto a small plate before removing the gloves she wore and dropping them into the trash bin under the counter. Tia moved to help herself to coffee from the coffeemaker before accepting the plated cookie from her friend and following her into the back office.

"So, I found something out this morning," Cookie said, hopping to sit on the desktop and swinging her feet. She waited until Tia sat in the office chair before announcing her news. "Did you see the shop next door is finally available to rent?" She cocked her head to one side and gave Tia a hopeful, expectant look.

Tia's hand paused halfway to her mouth with the still warm cookie as her mouth dropped open in a small gasp. "Seriously? I didn't notice! Do you know what they're asking for rent?"

At Cookie's shake of her head, Tia placed the cookie back on the plate and pulled out her phone. "Who's got it listed? What's the number? Oh, never mind, I've got it." Her fingers slid on the phone's screen as she searched for the listing and pulled up the information. She and Cookie had discussed Tia's desire for studio space apart from her parents' house several times in the past couple of months. The shop next to the Gingersnap had been a jeweler's most recently, but had been empty for several weeks.

"Hmm. It says it's got one customer facing room, an office, a bathroom, and a large storage area." She nibbled on her bottom lip. "It would be perfect, but I don't know if I can swing that much."

Tia tried not to let disappointment sink her spirits. Of course, the listing would display the shop in the best light, but it really did seem like it would be perfect for her needs. Other than the price, which was a couple hundred more than she would like to spend each month.

"How do other artists manage to rent studios?" Cookie mused aloud and picked up a coffee cup that must have been on the desk from an earlier break and took a sip. "Can you get any ideas from your friends?"

Tia leaned back in Cookie's office chair and took a nibble of the cookie. Even distracted, she appreciated the slight crispness of the edges surrounding the warm and cozy layers of oatmeal in the cookie. She returned her mind to Cookie's question. "Well, some of them run their space as a community, where artists can rent space and time. Sort of like a hairdresser rents a chair in a salon, I guess. Some offer classes, depending on their projects."

She fell silent as she took another bite and thought through some options.

After a moment, she picked up her phone again. "You know what? I'm going to ask for a viewing. It can't hurt, right?"

Cookie grinned and clapped her hands under her chin. Her eyes twinkled as Tia sent an email to the real estate agent.

Chapter 2

Afternoon break concluded, Cookie walked Tia back to the front of the cafe. Nikola stood behind the counter, frowning and apparently absorbed in wiping the surface down, but Tia saw her dart quick glances toward the sitting area.

Tia lifted her brows and cocked her head in a questioning expression. Nikola caught the movement but returned the smallest of shakes of her head, her lips compressed. Her gaze shifted back to the scene in the other portion of the shop briefly before Cookie joined her behind the counter and Nikola turned back to the prep area behind her.

"You can't be serious!" The man's voice sounded dumbfounded, but soon turned angry. "You are, aren't you? We can't all live in your ideal world. Some people are just trying to make the best of a bad situation, and if I can help a little with that, I will. Don't use someone else's pain to fuel your campaign!"

Curiosity piqued, Tia took two steps so she could see past the support wall separating the counter area from the bookstore. A couple faced off in the center of the room; Tia recognized the man, though his hair was whiter and his frame a bit fuller than when she met him six years ago. He was Stuart Hamilton, one of the selectmen in town. Tia remembered him from the board when her mother was going through the permit application process to run Jenkins' Events.

"The people of this town voted these regulations for a reason, and it's not up to the good old boys to decide which rules they want to abide by and which don't apply to them!" The woman braced one fist on her slim hip and formed air quotes in front of Mr. Hamilton with the other, her bright red manicure punctuating her thoughts with passion. She wore her blonde hair slicked tightly back into a tiny bun at the nape of her neck. "You've been in this position too long when you think the voters don't deserve to know the truth!" Her voice rang loudly with conviction and tendons corded taut in her neck.

Mr. Hamilton snorted softly and shook his head. He turned away and scooped up some papers and a cup from a small table where he must have been sitting. Returning his attention to the woman, he softened his voice. "Please don't do this. It will only cause a good man to feel shame. Is that the kind of selectman you want to be?"

He didn't wait for her response. He noticed Tia staring on his way to the door and gave a short nod. The tight smile he offered didn't reach his eyes.

Tia's attention returned to the other room in time to see the woman's shift in posture; her shoulders squared and her chin lifting an inch or so as though readying for battle. She smiled at Tia and strode forward.

"Hello! I'm Kiera D'Eath. I'm sure you've seen my signs; I'm running for a seat on the Board of Selectman in the election at the end of the month, and I'd appreciate your vote!" She held out her hand, waiting for Tia to juggle her tote bag so she could shake it.

She was right, Tia had seen the signs. Bright red with white lettering, they were staked in yards all around town. "Vote Kiera D'Eath (D'EEth), selectman". She nodded and shifted her bag back to her reclaimed hand. "Yes, I've seen them. You have an interesting last name."

Kiera's smile was wide and bright. "I know, it threw me the first time I saw it written out because it looks like it would be pronounced differently. My husband's family have traced their ancestors back to Britain in the 1200s! There are so many fascinating stories about the possible origins of the surname. I lean toward the one that says they were from the town of Ath in Belgium, but there's also one that suggests they sold kindling for fires."

Tia nodded and tried to school her face into reflecting interest instead of an urgent need to hit the down button on the woman's boisterous volume.

"There will be a candidate forum at the Council of Aging the Monday following the Spring Fling. I encourage everyone to attend and bring your questions. After all, informed voters make the best decisions, don't they? I hope to see you there!" She turned the wattage on her smile up still further, waving a jaunty farewell before sailing out the door.

Tia turned to meet Cookie's eyes. At the mirth bubbling up on Cookie's face, Tia knew her expression betrayed how flabbergasted the brief exchange had left her.

"Wow."

Cookie and Nikola actually laughed.

"She's a lot, huh?" Cookie's smile ebbed as she thought about the scene they had witnessed. "Stuart Hamilton meets people in the reading room sometimes. He's always professional, from what I've seen. I wonder what she thinks he's done that's so bad."

Nikola shook her platinum head as she finished restocking sugar packets into a basket on the counter. "He was sitting there drinking his coffee and reading some papers when she came in.

I didn't hear everything, but she said something about Chuck White. I think that might be who Stuart has been helping."

Tia turned her puzzled gaze back to Cookie. Before she could ask, Cookie clarified.

"An older guy, lives in Saltbox village. Kind of down and out. I think he's a veteran."

It meant nothing to Tia. At the sound of the bell's jingle, she shrugged and made her exit as Cookie's attention shifted to her new patrons.

***

Tia juggled trying to set the purchases on the kitchen counter as she reached for her phone in its pocket in her purse. The plastic shopping bags had twisted around her fingers and were now slowly turning her skin purple as the weight of the contents combined to cut off her circulation.

She lost the battle. The tune emanating from her phone ended as she finally freed it from its pocket. She let out a growl of frustration and maneuvered the bags firmly onto the counter, wincing as she released her hold and wiggled her fingers loose.

"Tia is angry?" The soft voice came from the corner of the room.

Tia scanned the kitchen for Meela, biting her bottom lip as she found the Nowbi peeking shyly around the legs of a stool at the breakfast bar. Meela's furry ears were folded back, a sure indication that Tia's mood had frightened her.

"Oh, no, Meela, I'm not angry. I was just trying to answer my phone, but I missed the call." Tia crouched so that she wasn't towering over the little cat-hybrid and offered a gentle smile.

Meela nodded and released the leg of the stool she was gripping. She eased into the room, her large green eyes losing their wariness and returning to their normal spark of good humor.

"Beth asked Meela to care for packages Tia is bringing home." She opened a cabinet door under the counter Tia had put the bags on and slid a small set of steps out. Scampering up the steps and onto the counter, she helped herself to one of the bags and began emptying its contents onto the counter next to her.

"Oh, Meela, you don't have to," Tia began, but the Nowbi's wounded expression and drooping shoulders stopped her. "But, if you want to, I'd love that," she amended.

Meela's ears pricked up instantly, and she began humming as she resumed emptying the bags.

Tia's brows climbed her forehead in bemusement. Meela had approached Tia's parents a couple of years ago, asking to stay with them, and now was an integral part of the household. Having just recently moved back home, Tia was still unused to having someone so eager to clean up after her. The fact that the Nowbi was the size of a human toddler and her face was so expressive made Tia want to look after her, rather than the other way around.

A chime from the cell phone still in her hand caught Tia's attention, and she swiped the screen to see that the caller had left a message. Quickly playing the recording, she smiled. She still wasn't sure she'd be able to swing the rent, but she had the germ of an idea for a way that would allow her to generate the income she'd need while still leaving time for her own art. And now, she had an appointment to see the space to see if it would work. She checked her watch.

"Meela, do you know where my mother is? I've got an appointment, and I've told some shopkeepers I'll be there this evening to collect supplies. I need to let her know I'll be home later."

Meela turned from where she stood on the counter, stretching into one of the cabinets putting the shopping away. The tip of her fluffy tail waved behind her as it curled from under her skirt. "Oh, Beth and Jeff walked to the beach. They might bring Meela a conch, if they find one."

Tia nodded, already rummaging in a drawer for a pen. She scribbled a note on the pad of paper near the fridge and headed back out the door.

***

A dark-haired man stood in front of the open door of the shop. He wore a navy blue suit jacket over tan slacks and a dress shirt, but the top button of the shirt was undone and any tie he may have worn earlier in the day had since been discarded.

At first glance, Tia estimated his age to be within a few years of hers, maybe early 30s. He was clearly doing better in life, though. He looked fit and well groomed, whereas she...Tia peeked at her reflection in one of the store windows she passed and grimaced. She resisted the urge to smooth her hair. She wasn't here for a date; she was here to see whether she'd be able to take on the shop as studio space.

When she drew within distance that she didn't have to raise her voice, Tia smiled and hailed the man. "Luke?"

The man flashed a wide, toothy grin and stepped forward to meet her with an outstretched hand. "I'm Luke Garcia, with Garcia Family Real Estate. You must be Tia!" He paused just long enough for Tia's head to dip in the beginning of a nod before continuing. "I'm glad you got in touch about this storefront; you've got a great eye! This just came on the market last night, in fact, and I'm sure it won't be available for long, especially at this price point! But here, why don't I show you the space, and we can talk about what it would take for you to take the jump into opening your shop right here!"

Wincing inwardly at the immediate rush to the hard-sell approach, Tia stepped through the open door in front of the real estate agent. Up close, she could see the weedy growth of his patchy chin strap beard. Tia squashed the fleeting thought that there were two strikes against him already with a mental shake. It didn't matter what he looked like, because he wasn't a date. He was here to show her the space available to rent!

The tour didn't take long. As the listing stated, there was one large salesroom, a small office, a large back room for storage, and what amounted to a small closet with a sink and toilet squashed into it. Tia could see where the jeweler's display cabinets had stood in the salesroom because of the marks left on the flooring, but the room was empty now. The back room had wooden shelves built into place along one wall, but was otherwise empty. Tia knew from making her recyclable material collections that the large steel door at the rear of the room offered an exit to the alley behind the shops, where all the dumpsters were kept and deliveries made.

Luke kept up a stream of glowing endorsements of the space, along with recommendations of how it could be utilized or best equipped, depending on what Tia was interested in using the space for.

"So, what is your interest in the shop? What sort of business do you have in mind?" Luke's warm brown eyes flitted past Tia, around the storeroom, and to the back door before his gaze returned to rest on her face. "I can set you up with cleaners, builders, fire system inspectors — whoever you need to get started, I've got people who can help you." He gestured with one hand to the showroom, indicating they should retrace their steps while watching expectantly for her response.

"I'm looking for studio space. I've got an E-commerce shop where I sell foraged and upcycled art, and I'm thinking of offering classes, too. The extra space would come in handy for that.

I'll have to take a good look at the numbers to see if I can make it work. When do I need to let you know?"

They were out on the sidewalk. Luke turned from securing the door and slid the keys into his pocket. "Well, as I said, I don't expect this property to be on the market for long. This is a prime commercial site, but we just posted the listing and put the sign in the window last night. We'll be in House Spotter, the free print magazine, Saturday, and that always brings a lot of traffic. I don't want to mislead you; I don't need an answer tonight, but I wouldn't wait long if you think you're interested."

***

Tia moved her car from the town's parking lot to the alley behind Main Street. She lifted the car's hatchback before heading to the back of the flower shop for the boxes Zinni had promised to leave for her. The woman had been true to her word; the stack of cardboard included some nice thick boxes, including one in a peculiar shade of purple that would lend itself nicely as an accent in one of Tia's sculptures.

After stowing the cardboard in the trunk, Tia scanned the rest of the shops. Trash pickup wasn't until the end of the week, but it wouldn't hurt to take a quick look through the dumpsters to see if there was anything else she could use. Especially if she was going to be offering classes. She headed for the back of the hardware store.

She found a few torn packages of various metal fasteners in the hardware store bin, and some broken pottery pieces behind Antique Collective Stalls, a shop that sublet areas inside to various antique dealers in the area. Skipping the salon, not wanting the overwhelming odor of the hair chemicals to pervade the air of her car's interior, and moving past the Gingersnap, she headed back to the flower shop to see if Zinni had dropped anything in the dumpster.

As she tried shifting a bag out of the way, Tia could feel it was caught on something and leaned into the bin to see what was holding it. A dark piece of elaborately curved metal lay on top. It looked like some sort of modern art home decor. It also looked heavy. She took hold of it with both hands, but quickly let go. *Gah!* The thing had something dark and a little tacky on it, and now, so did her hands.

Tia wrinkled her nose in distaste and stopped herself just before wiping her palms on her jeans. She only had so many decent pairs of jeans left because of that habit. She looked around for something to wipe the mess off on.

A few newspaper pages sat pinned to the ground by a corner of the bin. She crouched and scrubbed her hands on the paper, doing her best to remove the substance. Holding her hand out to inspect it, Tia scowled. Whatever this was, the old paper wasn't doing much to help get rid of it. She glanced around the corner of the dumpster to see if there was anything else she could use.

Her breath caught in her chest. A hand lay on the ground, surrounded by a dark puddle. Tia's mouth froze open in a gasp as her horrified gaze traveled over the perfectly manicured nails, past the wrist, and up the forearm extending from the space between the dumpster and the wall. Those nails looked familiar!

Crawling forward, her eyes traveled past the forearm to find the rest of the person. Her breath caught in her throat as she saw the lifeless eyes staring up at the sky, but she forced herself to reach out and feel for a pulse in the woman's neck.

She fumbled quickly in her back pocket for her cell phone. With trembling fingers, she managed to dial the emergency number without taking her eyes from the woman's face. Her voice hitched when the line was answered. "I've just...I've just found a body."

Chapter 3

Cookie poured an extra measure of sweetened milk foam on top of the mug before sliding it across the counter to where Tia sat propping her chin on her folded forearms, trying to keep her eyes open.

"Here, this has a double shot of espresso. You look like you didn't get a wink last night!"

Tia groaned. "It was horrible. Every time I thought I was tired enough to fall asleep, I'd see that hand sticking out again! I think I maybe did fall asleep, but then dreamed the body was following me — turning up dead behind cars in parking lots, in the next aisle at the grocery store; that sort of thing. I'm so exhausted I can barely move, but I can't sit still, either."

The bell jingled as the door swung inward and Cookie moved back to the register to take the new customer's order. Tia sat up, rolling her head to ease the fatigue in her neck. It felt good, even if it didn't wake her up. She took a sip of the coffee and waited as Cookie plated a cup of tea and three shortbread fingers. The customer, an older woman with purple-tipped hair Tia had seen laughing as she browsed in the card section of the Winking Mouse Drugstore two weeks ago, had selected a seat in the reading room. Cookie delivered the woman's selection to the table and returned to Tia.

"That sounds so horrible!" Cookie leaned onto the counter and offered a sympathetic grimace. "What happened after you called the police, though? You said something about recognizing her?"

Tia took another fortifying gulp of coffee, thankful for both the slight burning of the soft tissue inside her mouth as a distraction and the extra milk that prevented the burn from being worse. "It was Kiera D'Eath, the loud woman who was running for the board of selectmen! At first, I recognized her manicure from when she told me I should go to the candidate's forum — they were bright red." Tia shuddered, remembering the lifeless fingers curled up from the pale palm. "But when I tried to find a pulse, I recognized her face, too."

"Oh my goodness! Are you serious?" Cookie's eyes were round pools of shock as the words spilled from her lips. "How did she die, did they say?"

Tia shuddered again and clamped down the urge to bolt home for another shower. "They think someone hit her over the head with a metal sculpture. It was in the dumpster — that's what I found first. I picked it up. There was something sticky on it, and I was trying to wipe it off my hands without ruining another pair of jeans."

Cookie's mouth formed a perfect circle to mirror her eyes. "Get out! Oh, Tia!"

Tia nodded, closing her eyes against the horrible memory threatening to choke her. "I know. I had her blood on..." her voice trailed off in a gasp and she buried her face in her hands, once again fighting the tears that kept surfacing since last night. "My parents had to bring a change of clothes to the station because the police said the clothes I was wearing are evidence. And they took my fingerprints, to match the ones that are all over the sculpture..."

She chanced a peek at Cookie.

The look of horror on her face had only intensified. She opened and closed her mouth a few times before rallying her thoughts. "But, that's just to rule you out, right? I mean, they can't think you killed her!"

Tia grimaced and lifted one shoulder in a weary shrug. "They were talking to her husband when I left, but they told me not to leave town."

The door jingled its bell again. Two stylishly groomed women entered the shop and strode to the counter without breaking their thread of conversation. Cookie squeezed Tia's hand before moving into her position behind the counter.

"I know it's horrible; I'm just saying! It'll take a lot for you to make up what she used to spend."

The woman's eyes raked over Cookie's chalked menu boards as she spoke, her teeth flashing a gleaming white against the wine stain of her lipstick. Tia was mesmerized by the woman's hair, flowing in inky black waves halfway down her back. Hints of midnight blue or deep violet seemed to catch the light randomly throughout her tresses. She was oblivious to Tia's covert attention, continuing to state her opinion as she considered her menu options.

"Customers that regular are just so hard to come by. She might have been hard to please, but at least her money was good. I got her every couple of months for highlights, but she was in your chair at least every other week. Hey, have you ever tried the pumpkin swirl sticky chai here? I love chai, but I'm so over pumpkin."

The second woman shook her head, her eyes also scanning the menu items, but her response made it clear she wasn't focused on the offerings.

"She wasn't just hard to please, she was impossible. Smiling all the time, but it never seemed genuine. And did you ever see her hands? She was in yesterday afternoon to have me fix a nail she broke when she was opening her car door. She always needed them repaired. She could have done a medium oval shape and been able to actually use her hands, but she was obsessed with long stilettos." She sighed and tipped her head back, shaking her asymmetrical bob away from her face. "I'm going with a breve today, I think. I deserve it."

The first woman considered her friend and then the menu with raised eyebrows. "Too much cream for me. I thought you were cutting back?"

"Jessica, my client was just found, only a few hours after sitting in my chair, clubbed over the head with that ghastly statue Sophie insisted would make the salon 'avant-garde.'"

The sarcasm dripping from the final word suggested to Tia's ear that the nail tech's opinion didn't jibe with Sophie, the salon owner.

The woman lifted her chin defiantly and stepped up to the counter. "I'm going with the breve. I can start cutting back tomorrow."

The hair stylist quickly added her order for the sticky chai she'd been eying. As they waited for Cookie to create their drinks, the nail tech finally glanced down the counter and noticed Tia.

It was too late for Tia to pretend she hadn't been attuned to their conversation. She smiled apologetically and turned her gaze back to her coffee.

They could only have been talking about Kiera d'Eath. If she had been to the salon to get her nails repaired, it was probably after Tia had seen her at Cookie's. What else had she been up to before she was killed?

Tia's back pocket buzzed and she fished her phone out. She didn't recognize the number. The sudden sourness in her stomach made her regret the last sip of coffee she'd taken. She briefly considered letting the call go to voice-mail, but forced her trembling finger to swipe the screen.

"Hello?"

Her stomach knotted as the caller's voice requested her to make her way back to the police station. After confirming she would be there shortly, she ended the call.

"Are you okay? You look like you're about to pass out!" Cookie's eyes were filled with concern. "What was that call about?"

Tia tried to smile, but had to compress her lips to calm their quivering. She swallowed past a lump that had sprouted to the size of a small boulder in her throat, glancing around to find that the two women were already on their way down the sidewalk, and tried to keep her voice steady.

"The police want me to come back for some follow-up questions."

Cookie winced, then leaned closer. "Tia, you have nothing to be afraid of; you didn't kill her! This is nothing like before! You'll answer their questions, they'll clear you of suspicion, and you'll be ready to move in next door in time for Buttonwood Bay's Spring Fling!" Her voice was warm and supportive. "You are going to take it, aren't you?"

Tia groaned. "I didn't even have time to think about my budget last night! I would love to take it. The space would be perfect for a studio — there's plenty of storage space, and I could set up tables in the front room to offer classes. But there's a lot to do to make that happen..." she let her voice trail away.

Not to be dissuaded, Cookie's eyes brightened as though she'd already won. "All the more reason to get these questions out of the way so we can move onto the important stuff! We can get it ready for a soft opening, at least. It'd be a great way to introduce your studio to the town!"

Tia rolled her eyes and shook her head, but Cookie's tactic had worked. She was right; Tia hadn't killed Kiera d'Eath, so whatever these follow-up questions were, they would be easily put behind her. Promising to let Cookie know when she was done, Tia headed to the police station.

***

"Thank you for coming in."

Tia nodded, trying to draw in a deep breath as Detective Topher Montgomery stood behind his desk. He motioned for her to wait as he momentarily disappeared from her view through the thick glass, then a door on the side of the lobby opened and he stood back to invite her in.

She followed him down a corridor, past several doors, before he opened the last door in the hallway and gestured for her to enter. Inside the small room were two chairs set on either side of a table. Tia pulled out a chair and sat without being invited. She folded her hands together in her lap, forcing herself to sit still while she waited for the detective to begin.

"Tell me about what happened in Providence, Tia."

Tia's breath stuttered in her chest.

"What?" Tia's voice hitched, and she was back in the Providence police station, staring at the ink staining the chewed skin around her thumbnails as she sat alone in a quiet room, trying to understand how her life had come to that point.

She dragged in a lungful of the suddenly blighted air in the room.

Detective Montgomery's blue eyes pierced her with their intensity and Tia knew her reaction had betrayed her.

"You had to have known we would learn about the fire. Why don't you give me a rundown of what happened?"

Tia's hands were clammy. She pressed them to her legs, trying to keep from looking nervous. "There was a fire at my apartment; the fire inspector said it started in the stairway closet. They couldn't put it out, but they were able to prevent it from traveling to any other buildings."

She forced herself to meet Detective Montgomery's eyes.

"I was brought in for questioning, the same as my roommates and the tenants in the other two apartments. They ruled it as arson, but they never found who set it."

His eyes were steady, his face alert but giving nothing away. Tia waited, her nerves raw.

"So, what made you move back to Buttonwood Bay? Why not stay in Providence?"

Tia licked her lips with the tip of her tongue and stared into a corner of the room. "I had nowhere to stay. I lost everything in the fire."

"Okay, but surely there are agencies that would have put you up, gotten you started again. You had a decent job, right?"

She couldn't breathe. Her chest filled with an icy weight, threatening to drown her in despair again. She turned her heavy eyes back to Detective Montgomery.

"I lost my job the day before the fire."

"Tell me about that."

The words dropped from her lips in a monotone chain as she told of becoming suspicious of a coworker's tactics at the customer service center, uncovering discrepancies with some of the charges and refunds to accounts, and the subsequent confrontation with the coworker, when she unwittingly gave him enough time to go to their supervisor with manufactured evidence pointing to Tia as the perpetrator.

"I didn't do anything wrong. They even said they couldn't prove anything, but they fired both of us. I decided to come home and regroup."

"Know what this story reminds me of?" Detective Topher's eyebrows nearly formed a V over his glaring eyes. "This sounds like —"

"This is nothing like high school," Tia cut him off. "I swear, I didn't do anything wrong this time!"

He nodded, leaning forward and driving his index finger into the top of the desk as he made his points. "You see what I have here, don't you? First is a case of fraud, then arson, and now a murder. There may not have been enough to charge you in Providence, but you're up to your eyeballs in all three cases, aren't you?"

Chapter 4

Tia stirred the pot absently, her mind miles away in Providence rather than in her parents' kitchen trying to turn the last of the apples into sauce instead of tossing them because they'd gone soft.

It had taken a week before she'd been able to talk about the fire with her parents, and longer before she was able to explain what happened to her job. She had come crawling back to her childhood home and hid in her room for days, allowing her fear of disappointing her parents to magnify the trauma and keep her locked inside of her misery.

Her mother's insistence that Tia needed to come out to the living room to participate in life with the family finally broke through her despair.

Well, that, and Meela.

Now Tia felt like she was being dragged back under.

"Will Tia add cinnamon to the apples? Tia?"

The Nowbi's small hand tugging on the hem of Tia's sweatshirt finally penetrated Tia's musings. Glancing down at Meela's upturned face, Tia realized the Nowbi must have been asking for a few minutes.

"Oh, I'm sorry, Meela! I must have been woolgathering. I know you like cinnamon in your applesauce; of course I'll add it!" She mirrored the smile on Meela's face and returned her attention to the pot. Turning off the burner, she moved the pot to a trivet on the counter. "In fact, it's time for that now. Do you want to help?"

Meela pulled the steps from their spot under the counter and scampered up. She pulled the jar of ground cinnamon from its place in the cabinet and squatted near the pot. Tia smiled at her twitching ears, closed eyes, and enraptured expression as she leaned her face over the pot and deeply inhaled.

"Ready?"

Meela's eyes popped open and she nodded vigorously. A dimple appeared in one cheek with her quick smile. Carefully unscrewing the lid of the jar, she extended her hand and shook the cinnamon into the applesauce as delicately as though sprinkling fairy dust over growing tumblewillows. A soft sigh of contentment issued from her lips.

"Remember, though, we have to wait at least a little before we can taste it." Tia's caution brought a soft flush to Meela's cheeks. They both recalled the occasions Meela had been unable to resist and burned her mouth on the simmering sauce.

"Tia is such a wonderful cook. Meela is so happy Tia has come home and cooks for Meela." She crouched on the counter next to the pot, her fluffy tail wrapped around her feet while her nose sniffed the air blithely.

Tia goggled in surprise as Meela's comment sank in. "But, Mom cooks all the time, and I know you like her food!"

Meela nodded agreeably, a placid smile curving her pink lips. "Yes, Beth's food is tasty. Especially chicken! But Tia cooks Meela's favorites, and Tia lets Meela help." She lifted her face again, eyes closed and nose twitching as she inhaled the aromatic steam rising from the applesauce. "Meela likes to help."

Tia's mouth twisted in a small grimace. Her parents had surprised her when they'd accepted the Nowbi into their home in the first place, given her mother's strict adherence to cleanliness and food safety measures. Even without running her catering business from the house, her mother just wouldn't be capable of letting Meela prepare the food, or even climbing up and sitting on the counter while food was being prepared.

Nowbis thrived on being nestmakers. In most homes, that meant cooking and cleaning and making the home warm and welcoming. Meela had had to make do with cleaning and putting away the groceries when they came in. When Tia moved back to her parents' home, Meela had finally had someone to nurture and care for. Both of them had blossomed in the ensuing months.

Tia straightened her shoulders. She wasn't going to let this new development of finding Kiera's body derail her again.

"Well, I love making food you enjoy, and I love having you help!" She handed Meela the potato masher. "Could you smash up the apples? We can have a bowlful for an afternoon snack. I've got to look at some paperwork. I'm going to see if I can rent a space downtown."

Meela took the masher and slowly began moving it around in the pot. Her ears drooped, though, and her teeth worked her lower lip. "Tia is moving?" Her question was soft, but Tia heard the sadness in her words.

"Oh, no, Meela! I won't be moving for a while. This is for a studio for my artwork. I'm going to see whether teaching some classes will bring in enough money to afford the space next to the Gingersnap."

Meela's ears perked up and she began pouncing the masher through the apples more vigorously. "Tia's rooms would be nicer with less cardboard. With Tia still in them."

Tia smiled, shaking her head as she headed to her cardboard-filled room to grab her laptop. Meela wasn't wrong, but trust the Nowbi to state her feelings plainly. She brought the laptop back to work at the kitchen table, walking into the room in time to see Meela lift a spoon from the still-steaming pot.

"You'll burn yourself!"

Meela lifted too-innocent eyes to meet hers. Pouting, she emptied the spoon back into the pot and placed it on the spoon rest, untasted. She padded back down the steps and tugged out the stool next to Tia's chair at the table. Pulling herself up, she leaned into Tia's side.

Tia adjusted her arm as she had so many times to allow Mia's hands to hold herself close, and they set to work. Tia messaged friends in the art world, seeking both information and encouragement, and pulled up websites for programs similar to what she was considering to gauge pricing and content offered.

Meela pointed out sculptures and paintings she thought were pretty.

After a couple hours of project planning and crunching numbers, Tia sent her proposal to her mother's office printer. "Meela, I wasn't sure at first, but now I honestly believe this could work!"

The door leading to the garage opened with a soft swish.

Tia's eyes swept the kitchen counter and she stood, closing her laptop and moving to slide the steps back into their cupboard before her mother entered from the mudroom. She pulled out a bowl to pour the now-cooled applesauce into and quickly wiped down the counter while filling the pot with water to wash it.

Sounds from the laundry room told Tia her mother was washing the linens from her latest event. Sparing a glance at the pot as she turned the water off, she chose to let it soak a minute while she helped her mother unload the van.

"Mom?" She found her at the back of the van, heaving a glassware-filled tote onto a wheeled cart so she could bring it to the dishwasher at the back of the garage. "Here, I'll start a load," she offered. "How did it go?"

Her mother smiled her gratitude. She stood a moment, arching her shoulders and kneading her thumbs into the small of her back. "It was a lovely party. There aren't even that many dishes to do, since the nursing home insisted on using theirs. I only have the serving dishes I brought for aesthetics."

Tia worked quickly to load the crystal plates and bowls into the dishwasher's racks. "Oh, that's convenient. How old was the woman?"

"One hundred and two, and she was still pretty sharp! Deaf as a doorknob, but pretty good at reading lips!"

Crunching of tires on gravel had Tia turning her head. Her father guided his utility truck into his parking spot on the side of the garage and joined them at the back of the van in time to help carry the last of the totes inside to her mother's office.

"Long day?" Jeff asked, squeezing Beth's shoulders before grabbing his lunch box and heading to the kitchen. "Come in and sit a minute."

Tia remembered to grab the business proposal she'd drafted from the printer and followed them back to the kitchen.

Beth glanced at the pot in the sink as she flipped the switch to turn the electric kettle on for a cup of tea. "I see you made applesauce."

Tia nodded, moving to store the bowl of sauce in the refrigerator. "I did. I'll wash this up now. Do you guys have a few minutes? I wanted to run something by you." She made short work of the pan, since the water had already done most of the cleaning for her.

Beth popped a tea bag into a tall mug and poured the steaming water on top. She held the cup under her chin, inhaling deeply to pull the scented steam into her lungs. "I do. Is it something I can sit down for?"

Tia nodded, grabbing the pages she had placed on the counter and moving back to the table.

Her dad finished unpacking his box and put the ice packs in the freezer to be ready for the next morning. He stepped briefly into the mudroom before returning in his stocking feet. He pulled a chair out and sat across the table from Tia, rolling his neck and shoulders. Tia knew he always needed a few minutes to release the tension of the day from his body.

"How'd work go today?" She asked.

He smiled. "Not bad. I've got most of the racks fitted and Jack framed off the space for the cabinets today, so we'll be able to get the rest of the kitchen finished by the end of the week."

Her mother joined them, carrying her mug carefully to prevent spilling the hot tea. Tia slid the pages in front of them. Her mother's eyes skimmed the top page. She quickly scanned the next two pages, then returned to the first page and began again, slower. Beth passed the pages to Jeff as she finished them, and he examined them before handing them back to her.

Tia waited. Watching, barely breathing.

This would be a huge step. It would be taking a much different path than the one she'd traveled since college. She did have some savings, but this would use almost everything she had. It was risky. Her fingers curled with the urge to create, to sketch or paint — to make something big.

Beth put the pages down on the table. Her questioning eyes met Tia's. "I thought you always wanted to leave Buttonwood Bay?"

Tia frowned, considering. "You know, I couldn't wait to leave, when I was in school. But then I did leave, and I think my expectations of what life was like in the rest of the world were different than reality. And I found there was a lot about home that I missed while I was out there."

A smile bloomed on her mother's face.

Her father pulled the pages back and studied them. "You've got the money to put into this?"

Tia gave a tight nod, her lips pressed together and eyes bright.

"You've got to know that when the economy gets tight, extras like art are the first things to get cut from people's budgets," he cautioned, still scanning the pages. He flipped to the last page before meeting her eyes. "But it looks like a solid plan if you can get the students. Are you going to assess community interest before you rent the space?"

Tia bit her lip. "The building where the jewelry store used to be is available now. I'm afraid if I wait, it'll be gone. That location would be perfect for the classes."

He nodded slowly. "It's a risk." A soft grin surfaced. "But, then, we're a family of risk-takers, aren't we?"

Tia met their smiles with a wide smile of her own. They were behind her. She was going to do this!

She grabbed her phone to text Cookie.

Somehow, she had missed notification of a text. Her jaw fell open as she gasped. "The police took Zinnia Rosewood in for questioning!"

Chapter 5

T ia woke with a thrum of anticipation already running through her limbs. The conversation last night with her parents had covered the gamut of her ideas for her new venture. Tia hoped she would be able to take a salary from the studio soon, but her parents both urged caution, underpinned with the offer to live with them for the first year rent-free.

Now, it was time to get the storefront under agreement to lease before anyone else did. Quickly dressing in her usual jeans and t-shirt, Tia threw her hair into a messy bun and grabbed her phone and laptop. She quickly opened her phone to see if there were any updates on Zinnia, but there was nothing new.

"Mom! I'm heading to the Gingersnap!" Tia called as she scanned the living room for her sneakers.

"Beth has gone to the Flower Exchange. She left this letter for Tia." Meela padded softly into the room, holding up a page from the pad next to the fridge.

Tia smiled in thanks as she took the note and skimmed it. "Oh, Mom's got a planning meeting for the Spring Fling this afternoon. Do you need anything while I'm out, Meela?"

Meela shook her head. "Does Tia need Meela to help with anything today?" Her voice was wistful.

Tia hesitated. She didn't, but Meela seemed lonely. "Do you want to come with me? I'm going to show Cookie my plan, and hopefully sign the lease agreement. Then I've got to get started on some marketing ideas."

Meela paused before shaking her head again. "No. Meela will see Tia at home."

Frowning, Tia shoved her foot into the sneaker she'd finally located under the couch. Meela seemed so comfortable with the family that Tia had forgotten how uncomfortable Nowbis could be in public.

"All right," she said slowly. "Well, listen, I'll bring you back something delicious from Cookie's. I've got to go. I'll be home this afternoon."

Tia nosed her car out past the lilacs into the street, stopping short as a minivan wailed on the horn before zooming past.

"Try driving the speed limit, toadstool!" She snapped, scowling at the receding taillights. She swiveled her head to check for cars again before pulling onto the street and heading for town.

The town lot held few vehicles this morning. Tia chose a spot near a landscaped island, where the canopy of a row of the Buttonwood trees the town was named after would help shade her car. She grabbed her bag and headed for the Gingersnap, her steps lighter than they'd been in days.

Conversation floated down the sidewalk as she neared a small cluster of women crossing the sidewalk.

"I was planning to vote for her. I hadn't thought about using the library meeting space for our knitting club until she suggested it. She acted like she thought the townies wanted to keep all the secrets for themselves, but we'd never asked anyone. You don't know what you don't know, right?"

The speaker was the youngest of the three women heading into the Winking Mouse Drugstore. She held the door open for the other two. When she met Tia's gaze and gestured, Tia smiled and shook her head, indicating that she was continuing on down the sidewalk. One of the women inside picked up the thread of their conversation.

"I heard they questioned Hamilton about her murder! Apparently he —" The closing door cut off the rest of her comment.

Tia's eyes flew to the door, but her own face reflected back to her from the darkened glass window. She snapped her jaw shut and hurried along. Stuart Hamilton had been questioned? Did that mean the police were still investigating? Had they not arrested Zinnia, then?

She glanced across the street as she passed Zinnia's shop, the Green Thumb. There were no lights on inside. It was still early, of course, so the shop wouldn't be open yet, but Zinni was usually working in the back room before opening.

Should she offer a caring ear?

But maybe Zinni would prefer some alone time to gird her loins, so to speak, before the morning rush of too curious neighbors descended?

Tia shook her head and reminded herself of the list of tasks she had set for herself this morning. The police would sort this out. She finally had a way forward; she needed to stay focused. She could catch up with Zinnia once the initial frenzy had passed and Zinni had a moment to breathe.

Pushing open the door to the Gingersnap, Tia inhaled the scents of warm cinnamon, brown sugar, and coffee. Grinning, she headed straight for the counter to place her order.

Nikola straightened and slid the door closed on the display counter. Her smile was instant, though pinched. "Hey, Tia. What'll you have?"

Tia decided on a vanilla chai latte. "And I'll take a piece of that coffee cake, too," she added. "That smells amazing!"

Nikola's movements were sure, but the slump of her shoulders and the muted glimmer in place of the usual incandescent gleam of her skin revealed her fatigue.

"Busy day yesterday, or late night last night?" Tia quizzed.

Nikola's gaze flitted around the busy seating area before meeting Tia's eyes. "The police were around all day yesterday, asking everyone and their grandmother questions! They didn't make us close, but I almost wish they had. So many people were in, trying to get inside information or something." She exhaled in a gust, directing her breath to blow her platinum bangs from her eyes. "Cookie made extra batches of cookies and pastries, and we still ran out of almost everything!"

Tia craned her neck to try to see if Cookie was in the back, but Nikola shook her head. "She stayed late last night to get everything ready for me to open this morning, so she won't be in for another hour."

The bell on the door tinkled behind her. Tia nodded, smiling in commiseration at Nikola before taking her breakfast to one of the stools near the window. She pulled out her laptop and sent a quick message to Luke Garcia before settling back with her tea.

Her first sip was creamy and perfectly spiced with cardamom, ginger, cloves, and cinnamon. She sighed contentedly before piercing the tines of her fork through the decadently crumbly topping of the pale yellow cake. Lifting a bite to her lips, she closed her eyes to appreciate thoroughly the dance of flavors across her tongue.

Her portion disappeared too quickly. Tia realized she was going to have to start some kind of exercise program if she was going to be working next door to Cookie's temptations. She deposited the dish in the bus tub left near the door and returned to her laptop.

A flag of notification alerted her to Luke's reply. Tia skimmed the response and smiled, setting an alarm on her phone. He would meet her next door in twenty minutes.

She'd get the lease signed and be that much further along in her plans by the time she got to share the news with Cookie.

Tia opened a graphic program and searched through the images for something that would strike the right message for the "educational-and-creative-but-still-so-fun-children-would-beg-to-come" types of programs she planned to offer. She worked steadily on the poster until the alarm went off, uploaded it via email, then snapped her laptop closed.

Ginger still hadn't arrived. Tia waved to Nikola as she headed back to the sidewalk and quickly moved to wait in front of the front door of her new space. She gazed at the wide plate-glass windows, envisioning how she would display the studio name; "Artistic Adventures: Out of the Box Creations."

She hummed with happiness and tried to restrain the grin threatening to erupt. She wanted to present a professional front, didn't she? How professional would it be to be jumping around and grinning like a gleeful teenager?

Despite her self-chastisements, she spun around at Luke's reflection in the window crossing the street to meet her, her cheeks stretched wide in a grin.

His hair was still damp, curling back from his forehead. He reached out with a firm handshake. "You decided to take it! Congratulations! Let's get this paperwork filled out and get you approved!"

Tia nodded eagerly and waited for him to use his keys to open the door. The edge of a dinosaur-covered Band-Aid peeked out from under the suit jacket on his wrist, then he was sliding the keys back into his pants pocket and beckoning her to precede him into the store.

He opened his briefcase on one of the shelves in the back room and pulled out a sheaf of paperwork.

"Let's go over these so we can get you approved for the lease, then you can get excited about opening for business!" His smile was professional and efficient.

Tia nodded, reaching out to take the papers.

He held onto them. "Some of these can be confusing, so I like to go through them one at a time."

Tia suppressed a sigh and nodded agreeably. Her business degree made her fairly confident in her ability to understand the lease contract, but she didn't want to alienate Luke. She hoped to negotiate a reduction in the lease to allow her to get it set up and opened before paying the full price.

The next forty-five minutes was a dizzying shuffle of papers as Tia filled in form after form of financial information in addition to providing Luke with copies of her tax returns and the business plan she'd drafted.

Finally, he produced the lease agreement and reviewed the clauses. Essentially, Tia would be responsible for everything. It was what she had expected. She quickly scanned to see if there was a tenant improvement allowance. There wasn't.

She licked her lips, steeling herself to begin the negotiation.

Before she had gathered her nerve, Luke strolled toward the front window. He glanced up and down the sidewalk before turning and running his gaze around the shop.

"Do you have all the furnishings you'll need for your studio? I can set you up with a builder if you think you'll want more storage built in, or maybe units set up in the main room for displays? The last tenants did a decent enough job of cleaning the unit when they moved out, but I'm sure you'll want it professionally cleaned before moving in. I can help you get that set up."

Luke moved around the room, pointing out where the windows had collected dust on their sills and cobwebs collected in the corners near the ceiling.

Tia hesitated, then made a soft murmur of assent. She took the opportunity. "Oh, yes, I'm going to need to make improvements before I can run classes or anything. I don't see an improvement allowance in the lease. Is that something the landlord will consider?"

Luke was facing the sidewalk again. Did his posture stiffen? But no, he swung easily toward her, a ready smile in place.

"I'm glad you asked! The landlord is willing to knock a third off the rent for two months, but only when the tenant requests it. You've done your homework!"

He crossed back to his briefcase and withdrew another lease with the allowance already included. Tia carefully scanned this one, relieved that it had been so easy. She initialed the pages and signed the last sheet, then waited for Luke to scan it and email her a copy.

Smiling, he snapped the clasp on his briefcase. "So, I'll have the carpenter get in touch with you to see what you'll need, and you can work out your time frame with him. You'll want to wait to have it cleaned until he's done, I'm guessing."

Tia smiled. "Oh, I've got that covered, but thank you. My father's a carpenter, he's already agreed to help me."

Luke's smile flickered before he turned up the wattage. "Ah, good! There you go! Just let me know when you're ready for the cleaner, then!"

Tia smiled and accepted the keys he held out for her. The dinosaur-covered Band-Aid made its appearance again, and this time Tia allowed her amusement to show.

Luke followed her gaze and lifted one corner of his mouth in a smirk. "The neighbor's cat scratched me. Her son insisted I use one of his special bandages."

Tia's smile widened. "He must like you if he's willing to part with a dinosaur bandage!"

Out on the sidewalk, Tia bid Luke goodbye and turned to lock the door. Whispered scraping sounds nearby caught her attention, and she turned to see Zinnia crouched down, lettering her chalkboard sign in front of the Green Thumb.

"Zinnia!" Tia hurried over to see her. "How are you doing?"

Zinnia turned at Tia's approach. There were dark smudges under her eyes and her green hair was lank and lifeless. She tried for a smile, but the effort fell short.

"Hi, Tia. I'd like to say I'll be okay, but honestly, I've had better weeks."

Tia's chest was suddenly heavy, her throat tight. "I'm so sorry, Zinni." She reached out and brushed her hand on Zinnia's shoulder, wanting to offer comfort but unsure how.

Behind her, a brief disagreement sounded.

"But I want to look at the wind chimes!"

"Not today, Jace. Let's walk over here." A woman younger than Tia gripped the arm of a boy too small to be in school and pulled him across the street to the other sidewalk, carefully avoiding looking at Tia and Zinnia.

Zinnia let out a half sob. "I don't know if it's even worth opening the shop! That's one of the nicer reactions I've gotten." She closed her eyes and drew in a deep breath.

Tia's heart twisted. "But you didn't do anything wrong!"

Zinni opened her eyes and grimaced. "That may not be enough. Kiera D'Eath's body was found behind my store, with the murder weapon in my dumpster. I had closed early that afternoon for personal reasons, so my alibi is tenuous, according to Topher Montgomery." She shrugged weakly. "And Kiera blocked our purchase of a farm near the state forest because she wanted it for Conservation land, which some people think is motive."

She stood, indecisive, the fingers of one hand pulling and twisting at her spiritless hair. "I'm sorry. I think I'm just going to close for the day." She lifted the sign board and carried it back into the shop.

Tia allowed her feet to carry her back to the Gingersnap while she pondered Zinnia's story. Sighing, she tried to reason with herself.

She needed to let this go. She had so many things to do in the next few days if she wanted to be able to open for the Spring Fling, and since she'd just signed a three-year lease, that was important.

Glancing back at the closed sign in the window of The Green Thumb, she heaved a sigh.

But so was Zinnia.

Tia knew she hadn't killed Kiera.

Now, how could she prove it?

Chapter 6

The warm scent of baking brownies enveloped Tia as she opened the door of the Gingersnap. She caught Nikola's eye and raised one eyebrow in question. Nikola gestured with her head toward the kitchen, never missing a beat in ringing up her customer's order.

Tia maneuvered around the short line that had formed behind the couple at the counter trying to decide between bear claws topped with slivered almonds and sticky cinnamon buns and pushed open the swinging door to the kitchen. Cookie stood with her back to the door, peering into the closest oven.

Tia placed her bag on the counter just inside the door before stepping forward quietly and peering in, too. Chocolate chip cookies the size of her hand were just beginning to turn lightly golden around their edges.

"What are we watching for?" She whispered.

"Eek!" Cookie's shriek happened at the same time her hands shoved, and Tia found herself giggling maniacally on the floor. "Oh my goodness, Tia! You just about scared a year off my life!"

Cookie reached out with a hand to help Tia to her feet. Tia accepted the assist, grinning. A buzzer at the second oven sounded, followed quickly by a timer on Cookie's watch. Tia stepped back to allow Cookie access to the cookies and brownies she'd had in both ovens.

"Niki told me you were swamped yesterday. Looks like today is the same?"

Cookie nodded. She worked deftly to plate the cookies that were cooling on the racks from her last batch to make room for the new cookies. "Yes, still crazy busy. She said you were in earlier, though, and you had news. Spill!"

Tia's grin resurfaced. "I thought you might want to know, but now I'm wondering if I should keep it a surprise," she trailed off, raising her eyebrows at the warm cookies suggestively.

"Ha! I see how you are!" Cookie brandished her spatula in the air threateningly, but flourished it under an oatmeal raisin cookie that had broken in two and slid the pieces of cookie onto a napkin. "Pay up, first. You get your cookie when I get the deets."

Tia laughed. "Meela's cookie. I promised her a treat. But... guess who's going to be your neighbor?"

Cookie's eyes brightened. "You're taking the shop? Tia, that's awesome!"

Tia reached for the cookie and folded the napkin into a little package around it. "I just signed a three-year contract! I ran through my plan with my parents last night, and they've agreed to help where they can. Your suggestion to try to be open for the Spring Fling convinced me of my timeline." She tucked the cookie package safely into her purse.

Cookie's grin matched Tia's. "So glad I could be of service!" She shuffled the next two pans she had waiting into the ovens, deftly resetting the timers, before lifting a platter of cookies and moving toward the door. "Do you have a few minutes to sit? I hear the coffee in my office singing to me."

Tia jumped to hold the door open for Cookie to bring the platter through. "I do! I want to know what you've heard about the investigation, too. I can't believe the police think Zinnia could have done it."

"The police are following up on all available leads, not just Ms. Rosewood." The deep tone had Tia's head whipping around even as she realized her blunder. Detective Montgomery stood at the end of the display counter a few feet from the door, apparently waiting for his order.

"Detective!" Tia felt her face heating and knew she must be blushing. "Um, good morning!"

Cookie was already depositing the platter of fresh cookies behind the display case window. Tia wondered briefly how many espressos her friend had already consumed. Judging by her quick, efficient movements, Cookie would be running on fumes by the time she closed shop in the afternoon.

"I've got officers tracking down every witness' and suspects' story. Murder is a big allegation to make, and one we're going to be confident of before we make it. Are you sure your story is going to hold up?"

Detective Montgomery's back was to the rest of the shop, but even he could tell his words had made an impact by the room suddenly hushing around them. Tia watched a dull flush creep into his cheeks before Cookie's scowling face appeared behind him. She nudged Tia into the kitchen, letting the door swing shut in the detective's face.

Cookie headed straight for her office, pulling Tia along by the arm. "What. Was. That. About?" Cookie's eyes were wide.

Groaning, Tia said, "Remember when he wanted me to come back for more questioning yesterday?" At Cookie's quick nod, Tia continued. "He asked about what happened in Providence."

Cookie's face cleared. "Oh, well that's fine, right? Because you didn't start the fire! Of course your story is going to hold up. You know, the police were in here all day yesterday, and it looks like

they're going to be back again — I'm going to tell Uncle
Toffey I'm going to charge him rent if he's going to use my
shop for interviewing people!"

She looked like she meant right then and there.

Sighing, Tia reached out to stop her. Her friends knew
about the fire in Providence, but they'd recognized how
traumatized Tia had been and tried to help her move on from
it. She hadn't told them about her job. It had been easier to
just leave it in the past.

"It's not just the fire. I was let go from my job the day
before the fire. I found discrepancies and tracked them down
to one of my co-workers. I wanted to be sure, though, so
before I went to my supervisor, I talked to my co-worker."
She swallowed, willing herself not to get sucked into the
yawning pit of despair waiting for her.

"I was hoping I was wrong, that somehow he had just made
mistakes, not deliberate errors. I didn't want to be a snitch,
you know? But that gave him enough time to set me up,
instead. My supervisor didn't believe it, but in the end they
fired both of us. The next day my apartment burned." She
slumped on the edge of Cookie's desk. "Detective Montgomery said I'm up to my eyes in fraud, arson, and now
murder."

Cookie's mouth dropped open, momentarily stunned. Her
eyes searched Tia's intently before she nodded decisively.
"Okay, so how are we going to figure out who did do this,
then? That's all circumstantial evidence, and you didn't do
any of it. How do we figure out who did?"

Warmth bloomed in Tia's chest and her throat was suddenly tight. Her voice, when she had taken a moment to collect
herself, was husky. "Thank you."

A timer sounded from one of the ovens in the kitchen. "I got you!" Cookie pulled Tia into a fierce squeeze before hustling to move the cookies, calling over her shoulder, "I'll be right back."

Tia used the next few minutes to settle her nerves and recenter her thoughts. Cookie was right. Tia hadn't done any of the things Detective Montgomery was currently holding against her. The truth was on her side, despite her circumstances looking gloomy.

There were crucial differences between here and Providence, she realized. She hadn't been guilty of fraud any more than she was guilty of murder, but when the fire burned her apartment building, she hadn't found enough reason to stay and fight. She might have a history with Buttonwood Bay, but it was her home, and she wasn't fighting alone here.

Cookie bustled back into the office dusting her hands on her apron. "I've been thinking. So far, we know the police have questioned you and Zinnia Rosewood, and you're right. I don't believe Zinnia did this, either. But it could have been anyone else! How can we narrow it down?"

Tia frowned in thought. "I heard they questioned Stuart Hamilton, too. And, we know the sculpture came from the salon, so somehow that ties in. We can start with the people we know she interacted with. How often do people go in the alley?"

Cookie's eyes seemed to scan the ceiling as she considered Tia's question. "I mean, anyone can go back there, but usually only people with legitimate reasons do. Like, the trash collector, service people, deliveries. You. So, quite a few, but not compared to the whole town."

Tia nodded. "That's what I thought. So, we have to see if we can track her movements after she left here that afternoon."

Cookie hesitated, nodding slowly. "Okay, but how? The police won't let us look at the evidence they've collected or their interviews."

She was right, of course.

"No, we'll have to ask our own questions." Tia brightened as an idea came to her. "Hey, I'm trying to get my studio open in just a few weeks time. I need to see if I can put flyers up in the other shops. While I'm out I'll talk with the shop owners. Maybe I'll learn something."

Cookie nodded encouragingly. "That's good!" She finished off the remnants of the coffee she'd been nursing. "What about me? What should I do?"

Tia smiled. "You're in the perfect position for clues to come to you! Just keep your ears open — people say all sorts of things when they don't realize you're listening!"

Another timer sounded from an oven in the kitchen.

Tia used the interruption as her cue to start the next step in her business plan and headed to the printer to pick up her posters.

***

Tia stopped at the counter of Main Street Market first. She might as well be thorough and hit every shop on the street. She tacked the flyer for her studio on the community bulletin board just inside the doors, but none of the cashiers had seen Kiera D'Eath in weeks.

"I heard her husband did their shopping in Boston. There's a lot more options in the city, and they like a lot of stuff we don't carry. When they first moved here she came in, asking for things like 'fwa grah' and truffles. I never even heard of those, never mind knowin' anyone who would eat 'em!"

Tia smiled and shook her head in commiseration before heading next door to Merserves. The bakery didn't have a seating area, so Tia didn't expect much in the way of Kiera tracking. It was still worth a shot, though.

"Hey, did you know the woman who was found in the alley the other day?"

The young woman behind the register grimaced. "Yeah, she ordered from us all the time. She was supposed to pick up a couple of vegan tea cakes yesterday morning! Luckily, we were able to pivot and redecorate a little to sell those as cake slices." She gestured at the display case, where there were still two slices of pale yellow cake topped with lavender icing and a sugared pansy.

"Wow!" Tia bent to inspect the cakes before posing her next question. "She had a real sweet tooth, huh?"

"Oh, she wasn't eating them all herself. She had different orders depending on what meetings she was planning. I could always tell if she was going to the senior center, because she wanted low sugar recipes. She said she didn't want to contribute to anyone's diabetes."

"That makes sense," Tia mused, "she was running for election. I bet she was meeting with a lot of people to try to get votes." She checked her bag to make sure she had her flyers and tape. "How far ahead did she order the cakes?"

A bell rang in the back of the store. "Oh, she was in every week to order for the next. Look, I've got to go, I've got a delivery."

Tia thanked her with a wave and headed for the next shop on the street.

She paused to check for traffic at the entrance to the town's parking lot. A disheveled man wearing a ratty ball cap and well-worn jeans walked toward her, pushing a bicycle, but no vehicles approached.

Something about the man teased at Tia, though she was sure she'd never seen him.

"Chuck!" An older gentleman crossed the lawn of the town hall, hailing the bicycle-pusher with a raised arm as he did. "Chuck, I heard you finally went to the doctor Wednesday! Maria said she drove you over. Did he tell you to take more magnesium?"

Chuck had slowed his roll, but still proceeded toward the street. His mouth twitched in a way that Tia half expected him to growl, but he just grunted as the older man caught up to him.

"What'd he say about your headaches, Chuck?" The man didn't appear offended at the unkempt man's demeanor. "I assume you told him no pills?"

This time, Chuck did growl. "'Course I told him no pills! And he tried, anyway!" He harrumphed again before adding, "but he finally said to try feverfew or butterbur. I took some feverfew tea yesterday and the head was better this morning."

The two men rounded the drive onto the sidewalk in front of Tia, heading toward Merserves.

"So, it was worth the trip to the V.A. after all!" The older man's cheer was met with another grunt.

"Four hours just for him to tell me to drink some tea! It's no wonder the world's falling apart, it takes all afternoon to talk about a headache! I'd hate to have a real emergency!"

"But, your head's better now?"

"Yeah, it's better."

From his disgruntled tone, Tia thought he would have been happier if the tea hadn't worked. Moving past the town hall, she prodded her memory.

Hadn't Cookie said something about a down-and-out veteran?

Yes — the man Kiera D'Eath had argued with Stuart Hamilton about.

Was this the same man?

Chapter 7

Knowing she needed to get the flyers up in windows where parents would see them, Tia hit the shops on Center Street next.

The attendant at The Bubblette laundromat had never heard of Kiera, but she was sure there were plenty of children in the neighborhood who would be happy to have art lessons.

Tia skipped Mad Duke Diner because, despite being called a diner, it tended more toward singles and late night rendezvous than families. That, and maybe because there was a police officer visible through the window talking to one of the waiters.

A Pizza the Action let her tape her flyer in the window, but the hostess admitted she only knew there had been a murder because she read about it on her newsfeed.

Several more shops allowed her to place her flyer, but Tia didn't learn anything new about Kiera until she spoke with Marianne, the cashier at the Winking Mouse.

"You must have had quite the view of everything going on the last couple days," Tia picked up two candy bars and turned them over in her hands, internally weighing whether she wanted to pay for the temptation just to have a reason to be in front of the register.

"Dragon scales! It was like being on a movie set! The day they found her body, the police cars came roaring up with their lights flashing and their sirens going — I thought there must be something going down right then! But then it was hours and hours they had the sidewalk blocked off and they were keeping everyone away." Marianne's hands gestured wildly while she talked, pantomiming swooping down the street and lurching to a stop pointing at the Green Thumb across the street.

"I was shocked when they finally said who it was. I'd seen her storming her way over to Sophie's a couple hours before the police showed up, but I hadn't seen come back since. It wasn't even that busy, so I was surprised I missed her."

"Storming over?" Tia placed the candy on the counter and dug out her wallet. "I heard that she'd gone in to get her manicure fixed, but why would she be storming in for that?"

"No, she was here after she got her nail fixed. She said she was opening the car door and her hand slipped, and her nail just broke!" Marianne held out a hand, fingers splayed, and admired her own magenta tips. She pursed her lips in a moue of sympathetic dismay. "But this was probably an hour later. She might have been coming from The Brews Brothers', from where she crossed the street."

Marianne looked past Tia's shoulder and Tia realized a small line had queued behind her. Thanking Marianne and dropping the candy bars into her purse, Tia made her way back to the sidewalk.

So, Kiera had gone to the salon twice in the same afternoon? Why? Tia took a breath and lifted her chin. She was making some headway. She tucked the information away and moved on to see the tailor at Fit Sew Good to ask to tack up her flyer before stopping at The Brews Brothers'.

The walkway between the sidewalk and The Brews Brothers' front door was lined with lamp posts sporting hanging baskets of flowers and capped with fairy lanterns. Tia skirted a mossy projection that boasted a stone basin on a pedestal where a particularly rowdy group of pyskies were practicing dive bombing each other, casting water in great splashes onto the walkway. A wooden sign on a stake had been pulled from the ground and discarded on the ground nearby, stating "no pyskies" allowed.

The front door opened and a trio of men exited the pub, reaching the bottom of the stairs at the same time as Tia. She paused to let them move clear of the stairway. Stuart Hamilton brought up the rear of the group.

"Mr. Hamilton!" The words blurted from Tia's mouth before she had time to think of what might come next.

Mr. Hamilton's smile was non-committal, a practiced politician's gesture even as his eyes held just a hint of vague recollection. "What can I do for you?"

Tia winced, shaking her head in regret. "Sorry, I didn't mean to stop you. I saw you at the Gingersnap the other day with Kiera d'Eath." At his suddenly closed expression, she found herself stammering in explanation. "I was...I was the one who found her in the alley that afternoon."

The corners of his mouth turned down and his brows drew in. His voice was deep and quiet when he said, "I'm sorry, that must have been so difficult." His eyes flicked to the men now waiting for him just past the splash zone around the stone basin before returning to Tia. His hand touched her elbow lightly. "How are you holding up?"

Tia blinked the sudden moisture from her eyes at his unexpected kindness and forced a smile. "A little shaken, but I'll be okay. I'm opening an art studio next to the Gingersnap, so I'm going around putting up flyers." She fluttered the sheaf of flyers she held in her hand. "I'd like to be open in time for the Spring Fling."

Mr. Hamilton nodded encouragingly. "Good, good! It's probably best to keep busy!" His brows glided toward his receding hairline as he paused. "I don't recall hearing about this before; have you been in to file for permits? Sometimes it takes a while to get approval, depending on what the different boards have on their agendas."

Tia's eyes rounded. With all the excitement and distraction of the past few days, she had forgotten to check which permits she would need!

Reading her expression correctly, Mr. Hamilton pulled his sleeve back to check his watch. "If you go now, you've got time to pick up the applications, at least. The offices close at noon on Fridays, but you could at least get them ready to submit first thing Monday morning."

"Oh my gosh, thank you so much! I'm going now!" Flashing him a grateful smile, Tia did an about-face and hurried back to the town hall to check into the necessary permits.

***

Tia gazed at the board directing residents to the town's various boards and committee offices. If she wasn't sure what permits would be required, how was she supposed to know which boards she would have to visit? She thought back to her business classes and wished she had taken at least one of the entrepreneurial offerings instead of the extra human resource management courses.

Her mother had made appearances in front of several of the boards before she opened Jenkins' Events. Tia knew she wouldn't have to get permits for serving food, so mentally crossed that board off her list of potentials. Who else had her mother seen? She had a framed business certificate hanging on the wall in her home office. Which department would be responsible for those?

The door opened behind her.

"Hey, Tia! You're getting right into it, aren't you?" Luke Garcia's enthusiasm was contagious, and Tia found herself turning with a smile at his greeting.

"Well, I'm at least trying!" She grimaced in an exaggerated caricature of confusion. "I'm not sure what permits I need, though."

"Hmm. I'd start with the town clerk's office. She'll be able to tell you where else you need to go if you need something more than your business certificate." He gestured down the hall.

Tia smiled her thanks. "I was out putting up posters about the opening and ran into Stuart Hamilton. I'm so glad I did! With everything else going on after I found Kiera d'Eath, I had completely forgotten about permitting."

Luke's eyes snapped to Tia's face. "*You* found her?"

Tia bit her bottom lip, wincing. She probably shouldn't have revealed that. "Yeah," she admitted. She met his gaze. "Did you know her?"

Luke's face darkened. "We had met on a few occasions. She was running for election, so she made a point of attending meetings of different organizations around town to sway votes." He shrugged offhandedly and rearranged his face into a polite mask of indifference. "She accused quite a few businessmen of skirting laws, myself included. Probably accused that Kromera florist of something, too. It's a shame what happened, but I can't say I'm surprised."

There was something...off. Tia tried to unravel the inconsistency she detected without obviously questioning Luke's testimony. "Oh, wow. I bet accusing people of being shady would give a lot of people motive for wanting her dead."

Luke's eyebrows shot up. "Oh, no, I'm sure most people brushed it off. I know I did! I don't think many people took her too seriously. Still, the police have had most of the business owners downtown in for questioning about that afternoon. I told them, I was lining up jobs at a property on the West side of town most of the day, and I had to take my car to the car wash after pyskies dung-bombed it. Oh, and I showed you the property." He smiled warmly.

Tia pasted a smile on and took a few steps down the hall where Luke had gestured for the town clerk's office. "Right! Well, I need to get the papers for my permits before the office closes."

Luke nodded in dismissal. "Good luck!" He opened a door on the opposite wall and pulled it closed behind him. The sign over the door read "Board of Health."

Tia allowed her smile to fall as she hurried to the clerk's office. Was Luke saying he wasn't surprised someone had killed Kiera, or that he believed Zinnia was guilty? And what did he mean, Kiera had accused quite a few businessmen of skirting the law? What were they doing that she believed was illegal? What could she have accused them of?

She reached the clerk's office and gave a quick shake of her head, pushing those thoughts to the side. *Right.* She needed to get the papers to apply for her business certificate, and see if there were any other permits she would need.

Ten minutes later, Tia smiled her thanks again and stepped back into the hallway, tucking the folded packet of paperwork into her bag. She'd get these filled out this weekend and turn them in first thing on Monday. The clerk had assured her there would be no problem with getting it approved, since it didn't require a board meeting.

The clerk had said Tia shouldn't need any other permits, but now she hesitated. The way Mr. Hamilton had sounded, maybe she should just double check...

Voices around the corner drifted to her as she wavered over whether to stop in at the building department. "There wasn't anything for it, Andy. Stu called me to come take a look when he found out Chuck ran out of oil and was using those space heaters."

A lower voice muttered something Tia didn't catch, and the first voice shot back, "You've seen the inside of his place, Andy. That's a fire just waiting to happen. But when Stu and the boys pitched in to get the tank filled, they figured out the pipes had burst."

"So how did that pushy broad get involved? Chuck wouldn't hurt a fly, and you guys know he don't like people in his business. It's all right for you guys to be patting yourselves on the back; you helped some poor slob, aren't you great men of the community, but Chuck —"

The first man cut him off. "It wasn't like that, and you know it! Stuart was doing his best to keep it all quiet — why do you think she was bent out of shape? She was sure he was breaking some law because of how secretive he was being. Stu was looking at losing the election over this! How's that for patting himself on the back?"

Tia stepped back quickly as a red-faced man rounded the corner. The glower on his face didn't change when he saw her, nor did his pace. Tia offered a small smile, but she doubted he even noticed as he stormed out the door.

Tia frowned at the sign at the corner pointing the way to the building department down that hall. Maybe she could just take the clerk's word for it that she didn't need any other permits?

Steady footfalls sounded, quickly followed by a Lumini man exiting the hall. His short white hair stood up from his head as though he had run his hands through it, and his skin emitted the faint bioluminescent glow of his race. He nodded curtly at Tia as he passed her, and then he followed the first man through the door.

Tia stared pensively at the door, echoes of the argument running through her mind. She glanced back at the arrow to the planning board once, then she, too, headed for the door.

Chapter 8

Tia tied a knot in the brown twine and added the pack of cardboard she'd just tied together to the growing mountain of similar packs on the daybed. She'd been at it for a couple of hours now, and her rooms were finally beginning to look like more of a living area than a storage unit.

Turning, she surveyed the room. With her mother's begrudging consent, Tia had taken over her sister Evie's old room when she'd returned from Providence and ran out of space in her own room. The house was an old Cape with added dormers, and the girls had each had a bedroom of their own on the second floor, but neither room was large and the sloped ceilings limited the functional area even further. Without all the haphazard stacks and random collections of various materials Tia had collected for her upcycled art projects, the room was returning to the shabby-chic chamber Evie had left it.

Tia had to admit her own bedroom had never been quite as fashionable as Evie's, with Evie's tastes running more to muted pastels and neutral shades while Tia preferred happy splashes of color. However, for months, the overarching theme of both rooms had been the medium brown of cardboard, accented with blotches of paint and assorted plastic bottles and caps. She grinned. It felt good to be finally getting a separate space for her projects.

Right. With a decisive nod, she hoisted a stack of cardboard bundles and headed for the stairs. She wasn't sure how she wanted to set up the space yet, but the shelves in the storeroom would definitely be storage. The sooner she started turning the shop into a studio, the sooner it would start to pique interest around town, so she might as well get started.

Three trips up and down the stairs filled the back of her car. Tia ran back into the house to grab her keys. A gentle melody bubbled from the kitchen, stalling her steps. She cocked an ear toward the sound. Was her mother home? Tia stepped softly to the corner and peeked into the room.

Meela balanced on the top of the step stool in front of the sink and dipped a cotton dishcloth into a pile of suds, then scampered down and ran the wet cloth over the front of a cabinet door.

"Ain't she sweet? An' she's walking down the street, an' they ask you confident ally, ain't she sweet?" Meela added a hip bump at each pause, finishing the line with a swish of her tail and hopping in front of the next cabinet to continue the song.

Tia smiled. She had no idea Meela could channel her own jazz singer! Seeing Meela's swinging tail reminded her of the wrapped up cookie she'd brought home for her. Moving quietly so she didn't startle the Nowbi, Tia backed away from the corner and called out her name.

Meela's singing abruptly cut off.

"Tia?" Her hesitant voice was higher than it had been.

Tia grinned, but forced her tone into a casual cadence. "Meela, I have the sweet I promised you!" She grabbed her bag from the coat tree next to the door and fished inside for the napkin packet.

Meela's face appeared in the doorway, her cheeks pink under sparkling eyes. "Tia remembered?"

Tia allowed her smile to spread as she held out the packet. "I got this warm from Cookie's oven for you!"

Meela took the proffered napkin and held it to her nose, inhaling the scent of the oatmeal raisin cookie. Her tail twitched from side to side as she closed her eyes in bliss.

Tia grinned. It was so easy to make Meela happy.

"Hey, Meela. I know you didn't want to come to the Gingersnap earlier, but I'm going to bring some of my supplies to my new studio. I signed the lease this morning! It's empty at the moment...would you want to come and see it?" She held her breath.

Meela tipped her head to one side, eyes still closed. Her cheeks rounded as her lips curved in a slow smile before she opened her eyes and met Tia's gaze. "Meela would like to come."

Tia's grin returned. She motioned with her head to the garage. "I'll grab your booster and shift some boxes in the car!"

***

Tia eased the nose of her car into the beginning of the alley behind the shops on Main Street. Her hands were tight on the steering wheel and her stomach felt fluttery, but not in a fun, amusement-park-ride way. She swallowed.

"Tia is frightened?" Meela's round eyes were curious as she peered up at Tia's face. She perched on the child's booster in the passenger seat, her legs curled up at her side.

Tia glanced over quickly, offering a reassuring smile. "Not really." She lifted her foot from the brake pedal and allowed the car to move forward. "I guess I just realized I haven't been back here since I found Kiera d'Eath's body. It feels ... a little spooky."

Meela nodded at Tia's explanation and settled back. She hummed a little under her breath, and Tia recognized the tune as the same one she had been singing and dancing to earlier. Tia smirked at the memory while pointing the car to the back of the studio.

After parking, Tia popped the trunk open and pulled out the keys Luke had given her as she walked to the back door. There were no windows on these doors, which Tia supposed might make it harder to break into, should someone try. The door pulled open easily enough, but the doorstop that should have swung down to hold the door open was missing. She scanned the alley for a rock or something to use to prop open the door.

There was nothing nearby, and Tia couldn't bring herself to go near the Green Thumb's dumpster. She left the door ajar and headed further into the alley, surveying the ground for something to use. Just past The Gingersnap's bin, a few bricks lay dislodged from the border surrounding an abandoned foundation garden. Tia only hesitated a moment before helping herself. She would find something more permanent to use and return this to Cookie later.

"I don't know! I just think too many people are asking too many questions — no! I — oh shoot, I've gotta go."

The woman's voice came from further up the alley. Tia lifted her head but didn't see anyone. She peered around, even toward the mouth of the alley. There were no more voices, and after a moment's hesitation, she returned to the task at hand.

As she picked up a second brick just to be on the safe side, the corner of an envelope caught in the weeds of the former garden caught her eye. Cookie wasn't one for gardening, but she wasn't one for litter, either. Tia grabbed the envelope along with the bricks and carried them back toward her car.

Meela hopped down from the back of the car when Tia approached.

"This is Tia's studio?"

"Right through this door!" Tia pulled the door wide again and braced it open with the bricks. They slid a little, then held. She held out one arm and elaborately gestured for Meela to cross the threshold, before glancing at the envelope she still held.

Tia recognized it as a generic mailer of coupons from businesses in the area. On the backside was a handwritten list of names, several of whom Tia recognized. Sam Harvey was a plumber. Wade Brewer and Dan Rivers were carpenters her father talked about working on jobs around town. The list included Wilson's Painting and Lucky Cat Cleaning...had someone planning to have work done lost their list of contractors? She flipped it over to see if there was an address.

There was. Kiera d'Eath's.

Tia's breath caught. This couldn't be a coincidence. Had Kiera had this with her the day she died? Had Kiera lost this list during whatever struggle resulted in her death? Tia's mouth went dry. She scanned the alley before hurrying through the door.

"Tia is going to have more furniture?" Meela padded back to Tia from the front room. Her large eyes scanned into the corners of the high ceilings and the built-in shelving unit.

Tia smiled. "Oh yes, I'll have more furniture. C'mon, let me show you!" She placed the envelope onto the shelf she'd signed her lease on, anchoring it with a mason jar filled with acorn caps. She led the way to the front, pointing to where she envisioned the work tables and the display units would sit, talking through the concept she'd dreamed for the studio.

Returning to the storeroom, she waved at the shelves. "These are great, but obviously I'll need more storage. I'm thinking maybe some drawers or bins, you know, something to keep the smaller materials organized better." She grinned, her heart light. "I want a big work table back here, too, for my own projects. And," she eyed Meela, hesitating. "I was thinking, maybe a cozy little corner somewhere? Like, if you ever wanted to come hang out with me?"

Meela turned slowly, examining the empty space. "Meela could come?" She turned her face up to Tia's, a slow smile blossoming.

Tia nodded, her grin returning.

"Right. Let me get the stuff from the car!" She bounced out the door and grabbed an armful of cardboard.

Meela had managed to climb to the middle of the shelving unit and begun pushing the cardboard into a semblance of organization by the time Tia returned with a second load. Her tail was swishing back and forth again, and Tia thought she might have even seen her do another hip bump. Grinning, she headed back to get the rest of the cardboard.

A silver pickup truck rolled to a stop behind the flower shop. Tia glanced over, then paused on her way to the car. Zinnia opened the door on the passenger side of the truck and slid out, followed by a teenaged Kromera girl with dark skin and a mop of purple curls. Jacob, Zinnia's husband, eased himself from behind the wheel.

Zinnia handed a set of keys to the girl before walking to where Tia stood. The girl used the keys to unlock The Green Thumb's back door, and she and Jacob disappeared inside.

"Hey, Tia." The tears from earlier were gone, but the sparkle she'd always displayed was still missing. She looked as though she'd aged ten years since the body had been found.

Tia's eyes searched her friend's face. "What's going on? The police haven't..."

Zinnia shook her head. "No, but I'd rather be prepared. Plus, it'll be easier to take care of the plants at home until we decide whether I'm going to reopen."

Tia's eyes widened. "Oh, Zinni!" She touched Zinnia's arm. "Can I do anything to help you?"

Zinnia pressed her lips together and closed her eyes momentarily. Taking a quick breath, she steadied herself. "We're not emptying the shop now, just taking the plants. Holly — that's Jacob's daughter — will be checking on the store every so often. So, if you see her around, that's what's going on."

Tia nodded, giving her friend a tight smile. Zinni met her eyes and nodded before heading to the store to begin packing her plants.

***

Tia was arranging the last bundle of cardboard when she heard tapping on the front door. Peering around the corner, she saw Luke on the sidewalk in front of the shop.

Dusting her hands on her jeans, she twisted the lock and opened the door, offering a smile. "What brings you by?"

Luke strode to the center of the room, hands in his pockets as he surveyed the space. "Just wanted to check how you're settling in. Were you able to get your permits filed?"

"I did, thank you!" Tia smiled and gestured around. "Now I'm just starting to bring in supplies and plan the layout."

Luke nodded, wandering toward the back room. "Mind if I take a look? Sometimes tenants have questions about what modifications they can make."

"Uh, sure." Tia followed him into the storage area where Meela was still arranging cardboard on the shelves. Luke's presence seemed to make her nervous — she shrank back into the shadows of the upper shelves.

Luke's eyes swept the room, taking in the stacks of disassembled boxes as well as the envelope sitting on the shelf. He turned back to Tia with his usual smile.

"So, walk me through what you're thinking. Maybe I can help you brainstorm!"

Tia's smile was tight, and she tried to relax as she pointed vaguely to where she intended to add various storage units and her own work table before coercing him back to the front room with gestures and descriptions of the work spaces she envisioned for lessons. She kept her chatter bright but vague and was able to usher him back onto the sidewalk in ten minutes.

With one last smile and wave, Tia closed the door and firmly twisted the lock. She resisted the urge to hunch her shoulders as she hurried back to the storeroom, unable to shake the feeling oh his eyes between her shoulder blades.

"Meela? Are you okay?"

Tia frowned, scanning the room for her little friend. She wanted Meela to feel comfortable in the studio. Apparently that was going to mean keeping strangers away until they had a space Meela felt settled in.

"Meela?"

Tia crossed to the still open back door and surveyed the alley, finally locating Meela in the car.

"Let me just get my bag and keys, okay?" She offered a small smile, relieved when Meela responded in kind and nodded.

Rushing back to the storeroom, Tia grabbed her bag and skimmed the room for anything she was forgetting. She kicked the bricks out of the way and locked the door behind her, testing its security before climbing into the car.

"I'll get Dad to make your spot first." Tia watched Meela out of the corner of her eye as she started the car and backed around the Rosewoods' van. "If you still want to come with me."

Meela gazed out her window for a moment, and Tia's heart sank. She should have had a safe space for Meela before inviting her, in case something like this happened.

"Meela likes Tia's box house. Could Tia bring the box house to her studio?"

And just like that, Tia's heart was light again. "Oh, that's a perfect idea, Meela! I love it!"

Tia had built the small house out of recyclable cardboard, masking tape, glue, and other craft supplies. A flower box under one window was a repurposed tissue box, while foundation rocks had been crafted out of takeout beverage trays. It had taken her weeks to complete and was the initial project that led to Tia taking over Evie's bedroom.

Meela nodded, nestling into her seat. She smiled contentedly. "Meela will bring a pillow for inside. It will be cozy."

Tia focused on pulling out of the alley, easing the nose of the car past the sidewalk so she could clearly see any oncoming traffic.

As Tia waited for a pickup truck to roll by, her eyes passed over pedestrians on the sidewalk. There was another police officer standing on the sidewalk in front of the Winking Mouse drugstore, her hands braced over the thick belt at her waist. She craned her neck as she leaned backward a little, attentively observing the neighborhood.

Jessica, the hairstylist from the salon, walked briskly down the sidewalk. She paused in front of Luke's real estate office, checking her reflection in the window before pushing on the door and stepping inside.

Tia stilled, suddenly remembering the woman's earlier comments about Kiera in the Gingersnap. The stylist had seemed more concerned with how the death would affect her business than anything. What business did the stylist have with the real estate agent?

"Tia is worried?" Meela observed quietly from the passenger seat.

Tia realized she was staring, still blocking the alley. "Just thinking," she said, forcing a smile. She eased out onto the street, but her mind was racing. Luke's behavior at the studio — no, his whole visit, had been strange. Now the shallow stylist was popping in to his office. Something about the connection nagged at her.

Chapter 9

Morning sunlight dappled the floor as it filtered into the studio through the buttonwoods on the sidewalk out front. Tia stood in the center of the front room, gesturing as she explained her vision to her father.

"I'd like some display shelving along this wall and under the front windows." She gestured at the walls in question. "And then a few work tables with stools that can slide under when not in use."

Her father nodded, making notes on his pad. His eyes were already measuring. "Smart. What about the back room?"

"That's where I want to set up my own workspace, plus built-in storage with cubbies for different sizes of materials. And, a special corner for Meela. She asked me to bring the Burrow." Tia smiled, using the title they'd given the cardboard sculpture house.

Her father's eyes lit up. "So that's why she was humming this morning!" He walked to the back room, with Tia following. "Where are you thinking for the storage cubbies?"

Tia pointed at the far wall, then walked him through her ideas for the rest of the space. Glancing at the built-in shelves she'd signed the lease on, she added, "Oh, and maybe a desk, too. This shelf isn't ideally suited for that." She frowned, puzzled. There was something off...Oh!

"Dad?" Her voice came out a little high. "Have you seen an envelope anywhere?"

He scanned the floor while shaking his head. "No, why? What's wrong?"

"I found an envelope in the alley yesterday; it had Kiera D'Eath's address on it." Tia's heart began to race. "And a list of contractors on the back."

"It's probably just trash, Tia. You found it on the ground in the alley, where all the dumpsters are, right?"

Tia pressed her lips together. Her father wouldn't understand her need to unravel Kiera's murder, but it was an itch that wouldn't go away.

"I put it here when I was showing Meela around, underneath this jar of acorns." Tia ran her fingers along the dusty shelf. "Luke Garcia stopped by later..." she trailed off, remembering his wandering inspection of the back room.

Her father shrugged. "You could ask Meela if she moved it. You know how she loves to tidy things. Why don't we get a list going for the lumber store so I can get started on your storage units? I bet I can knock out most of it this weekend!"

Tia nodded enthusiastically. "That'd be amazing, Dad! The sooner it looks like a studio, the sooner it starts attracting attention."

***

Once her father compiled the list of supplies he would need to create Tia's studio storage system and headed to the lumberyard, Tia sent a roll of paper unfurling across the floor under the large front window and took out the paint and brushes she'd brought to the shop that morning.

Before long she had a "coming soon" banner painted, with bold, bright colors proclaiming the name she'd settled on for the studio: Artistic Adventures: Out of the Box Creations. She stepped back to consider her work, debating whether to add more flourishes along the outer edge. A figure moving past the window cast a shadow across the paper, catching Tia's attention.

A teenage girl, her hair a mass of purple coils, walked back from The Gingersnap. Tia recognized Jacob's daughter from yesterday at the flower shop.

"Hey, Holly!" Tia wrenched the door open and stuck her head out, calling down the sidewalk. "How is Zinni?"

Holly paused, shifting her weight uncertainly before backtracking to the studio. Her dark skin contrasted beautifully with her vibrant hair, but her expression was guarded. "Not great. She's gotten some calls, and this morning someone left a dead plant at the end of the driveway..." she trailed off, staring down at her shoes.

"Calls? What kind of calls?" Tia glanced up and down the sidewalk before she tugged Holly into the studio.

Holly let herself be moved. "Like, threatening ones. Saying she should stay closed for good." Holly wrapped her arms around herself. "Some people really think she killed that woman."

Tia's heart sank. "That's ridiculous! Zinni wouldn't hurt anyone."

"I know that!" Holly's voice rose in frustration. "But the police keep pushing for her alibi, and she won't tell them who she was with that afternoon because..." She stopped abruptly, eyes darting to Tia's face as she realized she was blabbing away.

"Because what?" Tia prompted gently.

Holly closed her eyes, but not before Tia saw tears welling. "Because of me." She swiped at her face, wiping away tears. "She was meeting with someone, trying to help me. That's why the shop was closed early. But she doesn't want anyone to know."

Tia swallowed uncomfortably. Her mind raced with questions, but she didn't know Holly nearly enough to get into her personal business. That the girl felt guilty about putting Zinnia in jeopardy was painfully clear, and Tia's heart broke for her.

"Okay." Tia patted Holly's arm awkwardly, wishing she could offer more comfort. "Well, I'm here if you guys need anything. Anything. And Holly? Thanks for telling me."

Holly nodded once before slipping back out to the sidewalk, leaving Tia with more questions than answers. She watched Holly slip back into the Green Thumb and shook her head. Maybe a coffee would help her figure things out. It certainly couldn't hurt.

The bell jingled as Tia pushed open the door to the Gingersnap, and scents of warm cinnamon, vanilla, and maple teased at her taste buds. Cookie was behind the counter restocking clean mugs. Her eyes brightened when she saw Tia.

"You've been painting!"

Tia winced, scanning herself for the tattletale paint. "I did a 'coming soon' banner for the window," she admitted.

Cookie laughed and passed her a wet paper towel. "You must have been pushing your hair behind your ear, you've got it on your cheek."

Tia accepted the towel and scrubbed the side of her face. When the towel came away with smears of red, she met Cookie's eyes with raised eyebrows.

Cookie nodded, smiling. "You got it. Hey, are you going to be here for a few minutes? Nikki's shift starts in about fifteen minutes, and I've got tea to spill."

Tia nodded, then quickly retracted that. "If you're free in fifteen, I'll hit the next couple of shops to see if they'll hang my flyer and come back. I want to ask at the Salon about Wednesday." She gave Cookie a pointed look as two more customers approached the counter.

"Perfect! I know Jessica is there, she was in earlier for tea. I'll see you in a few." Cookie met her gaze conspiratorially before turning a beaming smile on her patrons.

***

"Good morning! Do you have an appointment?" Sophie stood behind a counter manning the phone and the appointment book, looking nearly the same as she had when Tia was in high school. Her face had acquired a few lines, but her skin was still fabulous and the highlights in her hair expertly blended with the gray, cut in a slightly shaggy pixie cut.

"Hi, Sophie! I don't know if you remember me, I'm Tia Jenkins..."

Sophie searched Tia's face, a welcoming smile blossoming on her own. "Tia Jenkins! I haven't seen you in years! I heard you moved to Providence! What brings you in?"

Tia grinned at the warm reception. "I did move to Providence, but now I'm back. I'm opening an art studio next to the Gingersnap! I was hoping I could put a flyer up here to let people know."

"Sure, honey! There's a bulletin board over there. Let me know if you can't find a thumb tack."

Tia beamed her thanks and turned to look for the board. It was on the side wall of the salon, just a few feet from the shampoo sinks and their reclining chairs. The salon wasn't large; just two stylists worked the floor, with a side room for the nail technician and another for an esthetician. The esthetician's door was closed, with a sign directing clients to call a phone number to schedule an appointment.

Jessica swept the remnants of her last haircut from under her chair over to the front of a plastic box with a sensor on the front.

Within seconds, Tia heard a whirring sound, and the hair had been sucked into the box.

"Oh, now that's neat!"

Jessica turned at Tia's comment. "It's a touch-less vacuum system. It's very handy! I've even thought of getting one for my apartment." She gave a tinkling laugh.

The phone rang and Sophie answered, quickly becoming engrossed in conversation. Tia took a step closer to Jessica. "I'm surprised it isn't busier in here. Have you had any impact on business since the murder?"

Jessica's eyes widened fractionally and flitted to Sophie before she responded. "It is a little slow for a Saturday, but I don't think that has to do with the murder. Why would it? It's not like she was found near our dumpster."

Tia blinked. "No, but the sculpture was from here. And she was here that afternoon."

Jessica lifted her chin. "Yes, she was here for a nail repair with Cheyenne. And, like I told the police, Sophie wasn't here, so I had put the sculpture in the alley. Anyone could have used it."

Tia nodded, as though relieved for her, then tipped her head as though she'd just remembered something. "I saw her at the Gingersnap just after lunch. I know she was here for her nails after that, but I heard she came back a second time..."

Jessica looked taken aback, but rallied quickly. "Oh, right. She came back to discuss changing her hair style before the candidate's forum. She has thin hair so she keeps it short, but she was thinking about adding layers." She swept her own inky-black hair back over her shoulder and darted another glance in Sophie's direction.

Tia nodded, thinking. "Do you know what time that was?"

Jessica shrugged, her eyes sharp. "I don't know. Cheyenne was out for her break, so maybe around four? Why?"

Tia met her eyes again. "I was the one who found her body."
She gave an exaggerated shudder. "Just makes me wonder how
close I came to seeing it happen."

Jessica's mouth dropped open. "Oh, wow! And you're moving
in next to the flower shop and that Kromera woman they think
did it! Watch your back, I'd say. You never can tell with them,
can you?" Her eyes flicked to Sophie again, and she moved the
broom in her hands. "Well, I've got work to do. Good luck on
your opening!" Her smile was too bright, her eyes too shiny.

Tia smiled her thanks and allowed the excuse to pull the
stylist away. She moved back to the board and found a free push
pin, carefully tacking her flyer so that it didn't cover anything
else on the board.

Sophie had finished her phone call, but answered another as
Tia crossed to the door. Tia received an answering wave from
the salon owner as she headed back to Cookie's.

***

Nikola was dancing to the song coming from the cafe's speak-
ers and wiping down the work table behind the counter. Tia was
glad to see that her skin had its typical soft glow — she must
have finally gotten a good night's rest. Nikola turned at the door's
jingle and saw Tia. She grinned and jerked her head toward the
back, and Tia went through to Cookie's office.

Cookie sat at her desk reviewing an order sheet. At Tia's
arrival, she nudged a plated bear claw closer to the still steaming
cup at the edge of Tia's side of the desk and leaned back in her
chair, wrinkling her nose at the familiar squeal of its springs.

"Ooh, thanks!" Tia grabbed a folding chair from behind the
door and sat, deeply inhaling the scent of the coffee as she lifted
the cup to her face. "This smells amazing." She stared at the wall
above Cookie's head for a moment, trying to put the clues she'd
gathered in some kind of order.

"You know how you told me to keep my ears open? You weren't wrong! People forget service people even have ears, once they've given their order." Cookie furrowed her brow, and Tia thought she might be angry about that if it hadn't proven useful.

"So, what'd you hear?"

Leaning forward, Cookie's eyes grew animated. "Billy Witt was on the phone this morning — which is so rude, by the way, ordering while still on the phone. Just hang up, already! Anyhow, he was talking about someone looking into all the permits the town's been issuing. Like, who was doing what jobs. I didn't follow all of it, but he said he thought something might come of it, but now that's a mute point — that's what he said, mute," she smirked, but continued without pausing for breath, "because now it'll get dropped and everything'll be same-old, same-old, and he's lucky he's getting the jobs he does land."

Tia frowned, trying to follow Cookie's description of the one-sided conversation. "I know Billy Witt, he's done jobs with my dad," she said slowly. "It sounds like he was saying there's been something shady going on with permits that have been issued. Did he think Kiera was investigating it?" Her eyes grew wide. "Do you think Stuart is involved? Was that what the fight was about?"

Cookie shrugged unhelpfully. "Ain't that the downside of gossip — you don't get the whole story?"

Tia picked at the bear claw, which was still warm from the oven, before sighing and pushing it aside. She wanted to be able to appreciate it, but her tension made it tasteless.

She brought Cookie up to speed on the clues she'd encountered since heading out to get her flyers, only omitting what Holly had told her this morning about Zinnia's alibi. As far as

Tia was concerned, Zinnia wasn't a suspect, so her meeting to help Holly wasn't a clue.

Cookie threw her head back and stared up at the ceiling. "So, who do we even have as suspects?"

Tia sighed. "There's too much information in my head! Every time I think I see the answer, something comes up to point at someone else. I need to write it down."

Cookie yanked open the paper drawer of her printer and pulled out a few sheets of copy paper. "Use this!"

Tia leaned forward and grabbed a pen, then started making a list:

- Kiera argued with Stuart Hamilton about Chuck White
- Luke said she accused businessmen of illegal activities
- Stuart risked the election to help fix Chuck's heat
- Chuck is very private
- Chuck was at a medical appointment
- Kiera had a list of contractors with her
- Someone was looking into permits being issued
- Kiera went to the salon a second time around 4
- Jessica was alone with Kiera at the salon
- Luke was at the studio, envelope is missing
- Jessica went to Luke's office right after he left my studio

Something was connecting these pieces, but Tia couldn't quite see the pattern yet. She needed more information.

Cookie's eyes widened. "Oh! That reminds me - I heard Cheyenne say something interesting yesterday. She was in here with the woman who does the facials. Apparently, Jessica was mopping the floor Wednesday afternoon when Cheyenne got back from her break. Jessica said she'd spilled some bleach. The way they were talking, it is *highly* unusual for Jessica to do any cleaning."

Tia added it to her list, then sat back, staring at the paper. "Cookie, it has to be Jessica! Look, she admitted she was alone with Kiera around four, and then Cheyenne finds her cleaning the floor with bleach? She called Zinni 'that Kromera woman,' which is gross, and she said she put the sculpture in the alley, but can anyone back that up? What if she hit Kiera with the sculpture and dragged her body out by Zinni's dumpster to frame her? And she was cleaning up the mess when Cheyenne came back!" She was out of breath.

Cookie drummed her fingers on the table, staring at the list upside down. "But, why? What motive did she have?"

Tia slumped back, frowning. There was a connection here, there had to be. What was it? She thought about each clue on the list.

"I think we cross Chuck White off the list. He wasn't any-where around. I wish we knew more about the contractors...." A sudden thought occurred to Tia. "What's Jessica's last name?"

As Cookie shook her head, Tia grabbed her phone and searched for the salon's website. "Jessica Rivers! I heard some-one talking in the alley when I found the envelope. Cookie, I bet she's connected to Dan Rivers — and he was one of the contractors on that envelope! That's her motive!" Tia scribbled Jessica's name on the paper and underlined it twice. "Then Luke saw the envelope in my studio and stole it for her. She must have been picking it up from his office when I saw her! It was her, Cookie, it had to be!"

Chapter 10

T ia pushed the remaining bit of French toast around her plate, gathering the last drops of maple syrup. Sunday brunch after church was one of her favorite traditions, especially since moving back home. Her mother had outdone herself this morning with puffy slices of brioche French toast, freshly sliced strawberries, and thick-cut bacon.

Meela perched on her booster seat next to Tia, carefully cutting her French toast into precise, tiny squares before dabbing each piece in syrup and popping it in her mouth. Her tail swished contentedly behind her and she hummed contentedly with each bite.

"I asked Kit Bailey to service the studio's HVAC system tomorrow," her father said, taking a sip of his coffee. "I'd like it done before you open. He said he can be there around noon, if that's good."

Mom set her empty juice glass down. "I was thinking, I've got some old shelves in the basement you might be able to use for displays, at least until you can afford exactly what you want."

Tia perked up, at once interested. "Yes, please! Recycling is my theme, remember? And noon is fine, Dad. I'll be there."

Tia's phone buzzed against the table. Cookie's name lit up the screen. Tia carried her plate to the dishwasher as she swiped to answer.

"Hey, Cookie! How's your day going?"

The silence on the other end made Tia's smile fade. When Cookie finally spoke, her voice was tight with tension..

"Tia. They found Jessica Rivers this morning."

Ice dropped down Tia's spine. "What? What do you mean, they found her?"

"In her apartment. They're saying...they're saying it looks like suicide." Cookie's voice cracked.

Tia gripped the phone tighter, aware of her parents' concerned looks. "Are you sure?"

"Yes. Sophie was here when Cheyenne called her. She said there was a bottle of pills, and a note confessing to killing Kiera. Ugh! Tia, I feel horrible. Cheyenne said they had plans to go to lunch and the movies today."

Tia's mind raced. They'd just pieced together Jessica's involvement yesterday. And now she was dead?

"I'll be right there." Tia ended the call and looked at her worried family. "I have to go. Jessica Rivers is dead. They're saying it looks like suicide."

Her father's fork froze in mid-air, the second helping of French toast suspended over his plate.. "The one you thought killed Kiera?"

Tia nodded, already standing. "I'm going to see Cookie."

***

The Gingersnap was subdued when Tia arrived. Even the usual Sunday morning regulars were quiet, huddled over their coffee cups and speaking in hushed tones. Cookie waved her through to the back office immediately.

"I've been thinking," Cookie said as soon as the door closed behind them. "Something's off about all this. Cheyenne said Jessica's apartment was too neat."

Tia frowned. "What do you mean, too neat?"

"Remember how Cheyenne said cleaning up wasn't really Jessica's style? Cheyenne told Sophie that when she got to Jessica's this morning, the kitchen and living room both seemed to have been wiped down. Jessica was on the couch in the living room, with an empty wine glass and a half-empty bottle of pills. Sophie doesn't think Jessica was taking any medicine."

"Wait." Tia's mind raced. "I thought you said they found a note?"

Cookie nodded quickly. "Yep, a typed suicide note. Jessica didn't have a printer." She huffed out a big breath, blowing her bangs upward. "Something else, though — Luke Garcia showed up at her apartment while the police were there. Apparently, she was his girlfriend."

"His girlfriend?" Tia's eyebrows shot up. "They were dating? Oh, Cookie, we didn't even consider that there might be a legitimate reason for Jessica going to his office!"

Tia closed her eyes and dropped her head. "I was so focused on Jessica because of the cleaning and the sculpture... but what if I got it wrong? Or... maybe she was cleaning because someone made her? What if...what if she was in on it with someone, or else she knew something?"

A knock at the office door made them both jump. Nikola poked her head in.

"Sorry to interrupt, but Detective Montgomery is here. He's asked to speak with both of you."

Tia's stomach clenched as she followed Cookie out front. The detective stood near the counter, his normally groomed salt and pepper hair looking more tousled than usual. His dark brown eyes examined Tia's face as she approached.

"Ladies. I understand you both spoke with Jessica Rivers recently?"

They nodded. Tia studied his expression, wondering if he believed the suicide story.

"Did either of you notice anything unusual about her behavior? Did she say or do anything that would suggest she was depressed or might harm herself?"

"Nope! She ran in yesterday to grab her tea before opening the salon yesterday," Cookie shrugged, shaking her head. "Nothing stood out to me. Sorry."

"Actually," Tia said slowly, "she seemed nervous, more than depressed. Especially when talking about Kiera's visits to the salon that day. She kept checking to make sure Sophie was busy."

Detective Montgomery's eyebrows rose. "Why were you talking to her about Ms. d'Eath's visits to the salon?"

Tia lifted her chin. "Because Zinnia Rosewood didn't do it, and I want to help her. She's been getting threats."

The detective's fists settled on his hips, and Tia could see muscles in his jaw clenching as he took a deep breath. "Might I remind you that this is still an active investigation? Ms. Rosewood is not the only person we have brought in for questioning, and she's not the only lead we are following up on." His eyes drilled into Tia's. "Better to tend your own Droplets than looking after everyone else's."

Tia mouth dropped open before she narrowed her eyes. "I am one hundred percent certain that I did not kill Kiera d'Eath. And if your theories include me or Zinni having anything to do with her murder, you've been kissing Dirmites!"

"So, we'll let you know if we think of anything else we might have seen, Uncle Toffey!" Cookie interrupted, grabbing Tia's wrist and tugging her toward the kitchen. "We've got to get back to our, ah, project."

Tia let herself be pulled, curling her lip in irritation. As the door swung closed behind them, neatly stopping Detective Montgomery's retort, she bared her teeth and growled.

"I know, Luv, but you won't help anyone if you get yourself thrown in jail for impeding an investigation again," Cookie soothed. "C'mon. I've got a week's menu to plan. What do you think, lemon bars or Biscoff cheesecake bites?"

Tia rolled her eyes at her friend's obvious distraction technique. "Is it supposed to take the place of oatmeal cookies?" she groused. "Because nothing beats your oatmeal cookies. If it's extra...your lemon bars are pretty spectacular." She gave a half-hearted smile to let Cookie know she appreciated her. "I'm gonna pop out the back and go to the studio. Dad's already started on the storage units."

Cookie nodded and returned her smile. "I'll let you know if I hear anything."

***

Tia walked through the propped open back door of the studio, the scent of freshly cut wood sharp in the air. Open shelves and cubbies lined two of the walls, with scraps of the lumber her father had used to build them already mounded in the center of the room for Tia to organize for future projects. As she moved deeper into the room, the volume of sound from neighboring shops faded, replaced by the soft rasp of her footsteps over the concrete floor.

"Sweetheart?" Her father's voice interrupted her inspection of the new storage, his brow lightly furrowed from concentration. "How's the layout feeling?"

"It's perfect, Dad! I can't believe you already got this much done!" She beamed at him, her spirits lifting amidst the unease swirling in her mind.

"Well, we don't have much time if you want to be open for the Spring Fling," he replied, wiping his hands on a rag. "Now, what about this hairdresser? I saw Topher on his way into the cafe. Are they ruling it a suicide?"

Tia sighed, tension folding over her shoulders as she recounted her clash with the detective. She winced and bit her lip before confessing, "I may have suggested he's been 'kissing Dirmites.'"

Her father's brow shot up, clearly surprised, and he blew out a breath, shaking his head. "It's your mouth that gets you into trouble, Tia. You can't accuse him of using hallucinogenics, even if he pushed your buttons."

"Yeah, I know, Dad!" Tia groaned, rubbing her temples. "It was just — telling me to 'tend my own Droplets,' Dad? He was rude first! I'm not some kid chasing magical chaos gremlins to see if I can get a wish — telling me to mind my own business while he's got me and Zinni on his suspect list is worse than rude, it's incompetent!"

He eyed Tia with compassion. "You were in Providence a long time. I know the culture is different there, but you have to remember where you are if you want this studio to succeed."

Tia's shoulders slumped and she heaved a sigh. "Dad, I didn't mean to insult him. I was just so angry!"

She felt his hands on her shoulders, rubbing away her chagrin. "I know, sweetheart. I know."

After a moment, Tia lifted her chin and gave her father a half-smile. "I'll watch my temper, I promise. I'm going to take some more flyers around and see if I can get the rest of the shops to let me put them up."

"I'll let you get on with it, then." Matching her smile, her father picked up his power drill and resumed the installation of her display shelves.

***

Tia paused outside the hardware store, her attention caught by a group of older men sitting on benches in front of the church next door.

"I heard they might not open the shop again. That'd be a shame, 'cuz Zinnia's got the best plant fertilizer around! She mixes it up special. It's what she uses on the plants she sells, but she'll sell you a five pound bag of the fertilizer if you ask."

"What do you use fertilizer for?"

The first man smirked. "Not me, my daughter. Sue's got a solarium on the side of her house nearly filled with plants. She's good with 'em, but she's even better with Zinnia's plant elixir. I buy it for her and bring it when I visit. It don't hurt to be the one in the know, does it? Kind of nice to still have her turn to me for something!"

Two of the other men chuckled. Tia turned and entered the hardware store, frowning. Was Zinni really thinking of closing up altogether, or was this just men shooting the breeze with idle gossip?

Harold Thorne, the stout, middle-aged owner of the store, lifted his eyes from the open newspaper on the counter as Tia approached and asked about posting her flyer. He took one and read it over carefully before nodding his assent.

"You can tape it up on the wall beside the door there. Do you need tape?"

It had been years since Tia had been in his store. Long enough that she'd forgotten how high Mr. Thorne's voice was, and her eyes widened in surprise. She quickly began rooting around in her bag, shaking her head while schooling her expression. "No, thank you. I brought some." Finding it, she hesitated. "You're the last shop on the alley. Did you notice anything unusual the day Kiera d'Eath's body was found?"

Mr. Thorne glanced toward the back of the store. "I hadn't seen a thing until the police arrived. I was out taking the day's trash out when they showed up. You know how it goes—working hard, not paying attention, and then suddenly there's chaos."

Tia leaned in closer, a flicker of interest sparking. "What about earlier in the afternoon?"

He rubbed the back of his neck. "Nah, not really. With just one clerk on, I don't have much down time. The girls next door would be the ones to talk to. Seems like they're always hanging out on their phones just inside the back door of the salon."

Her stomach twisted at the mention of the salon. "They found Jessica, one of the hairdressers, this morning. Dead. She swallowed before adding, "They said there was a note."

Mr. Thorne grimaced, shaking his head. "That's too bad. I wouldn't have said any of those girls were the type to do that." He blew out a breath. "I hope the police get it sorted soon. Town doesn't seem like it's in much of a celebratory mood at the moment. Understandable, of course, but...crass as this may be, it's not very good for business."

Tia nodded, thanked him for the use of his wall, and taped up her flyer before leaving in a somber state.

He was right. Tia hadn't seen much interest in the Spring Fling next week. All the conversations she'd overheard had been focused on the murder. And if Tia and Cookie were right, the murderer had just struck again.

Chapter 11

Tia tugged open the back door of the studio and kicked the bricks into place to hold it open before carting a file box of acrylic craft paints and carting it into the back room. The welcoming scent of fresh paint and wood shavings hung in the air from her father's marathon work session yesterday. His handiwork embellished the room, at once both functional and stylish. Tia grinned at the sight of the simple storage units awaiting her supplies. She set the box of paints on the counter and went back for a second load from the car.

A dozen trips later, she had various containers and stacks of colorful craft supplies piled around the storeroom. She loosely organized the materials where she intended to store them; several glass jars of colorful pompoms lined a shelf where they would catch the light from the front window, and a large wooden basket filled with assorted bits of cork sat beside a stack of old hardcover books Tia planned to disassemble. She stood back to assess. Hands clasped under her chin, she considered the space. She couldn't stop grinning as bubbles of excitement filled her chest — her dream was beginning to take shape!

Vocalizing the melody of a popular song stuck in her head despite not remembering any of the lyrics, Tia went back to the car and returned with The Burrow, the oversized house sculpture she'd made from boxes and recycled cardboard. Tia set the house on the wooden platform she'd asked her father to make, centering the porch near the front so that the inset steps on the side of the platform were hidden. The house served two purposes: Meela would be able to retreat to the house when she needed to, but it also added a touch of whimsy and artistic flair to the room.

There were still a lot of supplies at the house she planned to bring eventually, but she had enough to get started with. She planned a soft opening during the Spring Fling over the weekend. For that, she needed a simple but engaging activity that would attract both the kids she hoped to enroll in classes and the parents who would have to pay their tuitions.

Now she started assembling the activity's materials: bags filled with toilet paper and paper towel rolls, construction paper, paints, and shells. The sea creatures they'd make would be fun, adorable, and dry quickly enough to take with them the same day — all the things required for an introductory project!

Tia sat on a stool pulling cans of spray paint from a box on the floor and adding them to the shelf when she heard a knock at the open back door, followed by a familiar voice.

"Knock, knock! Mind if I peek?" Cookie's bright energy filled the space as she poked her head inside, her copper waves flowing freely over her shoulder without her ball cap to restrain them. Her blue eyes sparkled with good humor, a wide grin revealing her satisfaction at making Tia jump.

"Cookie!" Tia laughed, standing and motioning her in. "Come in! There's still a lot to do, but what do you think?."

Cookie scanned the studio, her face alight with interest. "Oh Tia! This is amazing! It's like a colorful dream exploded in here!" She slowly circled the room, taking in all the storage and the whimsical house now residing in the corner. "I can't believe you got all this done already!"

"Dad nearly pulled an all-nighter trying to finish it," Tia said. "Come through, look at the front room!" She tugged Cookie into the room where the classes would be held. Low shelves in front of the window waited to display student projects, while long tables and an eclectic assortment of stools stood in the center of the room. "I've got more projects at home to bring in for those," Tia gestured at several empty display shelves hanging on the walls. "I want to give a sampling of some of the types of classes I'll be offering."

Cookie wandered closer to a framed painting of a giraffe blowing a bubble, trailing her fingers over the table. A smile teased Tia's lips as her friend surveyed her progress. There was still a lot of work ahead of her, but she was energized for it.

Detective Montgomery strode past the large windows, a paper cup from the Gingersnap in his hand. Cookie's brow furrowed as her eyes followed him down the sidewalk. "So, funny story... Uncle Toffey was talking with one of the other officers at the café this morning."

Tia grimaced. "And?" she asked, apprehension creeping into her voice.

"He mentioned that if they don't uncover new evidence soon, they'll have no choice but to issue a warrant for Zinnia." Cookie's tone was low, the gravity of their friend's predicament weighing her words.

A wave of frustration surged through Tia, threatening to spill over. "What about the note they found with Jessica? For that matter, what about Jessica? Are they suggesting Zinni killed her, too?"

Cookie stepped closer, concern etched on her face. "Zinnia isn't around. They've got an officer watching the farm, but no one's seen her or Jacob since she closed the store Friday." She grimaced, then added, "They weren't looking until yesterday, but they think she might have tried to set Jessica up with the note and then scarpered."

Tia's pulse quickened as she absorbed Cookie's words. A quick glance through the windows revealed Detective Montgomery crossing the street, aiming for the Winking Mouse drugstore. She turned her focus back to Cookie, her lips twisting in mounting frustration.

"Zinnia wouldn't hurt anyone! She'd received threats. What if something happened to her? Or, what if she left because of the threats?" Tia couldn't stand still. She paced in front of the windows, absently cracking her knuckles. "There has to be a way to prove her innocence. Obviously the police don't have all the pieces."

Cookie nodded, but her brow was still furrowed in concern. "What are you thinking? You're not thinking of doing anything illegal, right?"

Tia sent a rueful smile at her bestie, shaking her head. "No. I've learned some caution since high school. Anything we uncover, we'll tell the police." She raked her fingers through her hair, then planted her fists on her hips. "We need to look at everything again. We were focused on Kiera and her last movements – we need to figure out where each suspect was that afternoon, and leading up to when Jessica was found. If we reconstruct the timeline right, maybe we can find a flaw — something the killer overlooked in their cover-up."

"Okay. Where do we start?"

Tia strode to the back room, grabbing a handful of markers from a cup on the way by. She pulled a large pad of newsprint paper to the middle of the worktable. "Write down our suspects at the top," she directed Cookie, as she rooted through her bag for the list of evidence they had compiled before landing on Jessica as the most likely candidate.

Cookie dragged a stool close to sit on and picked up a purple marker. "Okay, we had Stuart Hamilton, Chuck White, Zinnia," at Tia's exasperated tut, she explained, "I know, we don't think she did it, Tia, but if you want to find the real killer we have to look at everyone!"

Tia conceded with an irritated shrug, and Cookie continued.

"So, do we put Jessica down, even though she's dead?" At Tia's glare, she hurried on, writing quickly. "Okay, we include Jessica. Let's agree that we don't have to add you to the list. Is there anyone else we should include? I mean, she saw Cheyenne that day to have her nails done, and you said she was at the Brews Brothers before she went back to the salon..." Cookie groaned, her shoulders slumping. "Tia, this is impossible!"

"No, it isn't. There's no such thing as a perfect murder; the killer has to have made a mistake. And with two murders, the killer has made more mistakes. We just have to find one." Tia dragged another stool over to the table and laid the list of evidence down next to the pad in front of Cookie. "Somehow, we'll unravel this. Something ties this all together; we just have to figure out what."

Cookie bit her lip, staring at the names she'd written. She heaved a sigh. "Okay. Let's start with Chuck. What do we have on him? I know earlier you said we should cross him off the list."

Tia nodded, scanning the list of evidence. "Right, because he was at the VA for a headache all afternoon."

Cookie wrote VA under Chuck's name. "Do we know what time he came back?"

Tia frowned, considering. "No, we don't. He just said he was at the VA all afternoon. The other guy he was talking to said someone told him they had driven Chuck."

Cookie nodded, writing a question mark and the letters C O A. At Tia's raised eyebrows, she explained. "Well, the Council on Aging has volunteers that drive older folks to appointments or bring them meals. I don't think Chuck drives. He has a bicycle he uses around town, but he wouldn't take that to the VA. The closest one is where, Roxbury? Jamaica Plain? So, we can check the COA and see if someone from there drove him, and what time they got back."

Tia nodded, impressed. "Okay. It was right about six when I found her body, and Jessica said Kiera was in there sometime around four, so we're looking for someone unaccounted for in those two hours."

Cookie noted that down at the top of the page. "Okay, what about Zinnia? Do we know anything about her schedule that day?"

Tia sighed. "Well, I saw her out front of the shop on my way to the cafe. She said she was going to leave some cardboard for me that evening, which she did. That's why I was there in the first place, to get the boxes she put aside. See — why would she kill someone and leave their body behind her own dumpster when she knew I was going to be there in an hour or so?"

She grimaced and shook her head, irritated anew with the police investigation. "She said she closed the shop early for personal reasons, but Jacob's daughter, Holly, told me it was a meeting with someone to try to help Holly."

Cookie's eyes widened and her mouth momentarily dropped open before she spluttered, "Wait one minute! What do you mean, 'Jacob's daughter, Holly?' Since when does Jacob have a daughter?"

Tia tipped her head, frowning at Cookie. "Does he not have a daughter?" Her brow furrowed in concentration as she processed her thoughts. "I guess I only know Zinnia through the shop. I'd met Jacob a few times when I was in talking with Zinni. But, Friday afternoon, Holly was with them when they came to get plants to take home, and Zinni told me she was Jacob's daughter."

Cookie shook her head, her eyebrows climbing into her hairline. "I've known the Rosewoods for four years — since they moved here! They don't have any kids."

They stared at each other, disconcerted. Finally, Tia pointed at the list. "Better put Holly on there under Zinnia, then. I still can't believe Zinnia would hurt anyone. There has to be an explanation for all of this."

Cookie wrote Holly's name, underlined it, and added two question marks. Shaking her head, she added an exclamation mark with the other punctuation. "Okay, moving on for now..."

Tia's phone interrupted with an insistent buzzing. With an apologetic grimace at her friend, Tia fished the phone out of her pocket and answered.

"Hi, Mom! I'm at the studio, getting things organized." As her mother launched into her request, Tia glanced at her watch, rolling her eyes at Cookie and slumping onto her stool before replying. "Yeah, I can do that." She shook her head, her enthusiasm fizzling. "No, Mom, it's okay. It's fine." She straightened her back and lifted her shoulders, a silver lining presenting itself. "I'll zip home to get them, and see if Meela wants to come back here with me to help me organize the materials here."

Hanging up, she wrinkled her nose at Cookie. "Well, as you heard, that was an urgent plea for Tia's Delivery Service. Mom's got a Spring Fling meeting and forgot some of her files at home."

Cookie smiled, a dimple flashing in her cheek. "No problem. I've got the afternoon shift today. If you come up with anything good, stop in!"

Chapter 12

T ia parked on the street next to the library, noting that her
mother's van was parked in the lot across the street. The
library must be having story hour or something — the lot was
full, and Tia had only grabbed this spot because the car that had
been here pulled out as she arrived. Shutting the car off, Tia
turned to Meela, who perched in her booster, gazing intently
up into the branches of the Buttonwood that stretched out over
the sidewalk.

Tia leaned forward to see what had caught Meela's interest.
A pair of Pyskies, younger looking than the group in front of the
Brews Brothers had been, were engaged in a game of Fighting
Flamingos. Tia had seen the game played before, with both
players using just one arm and the opposite leg, each hopping
about and trying to get a ribbon or flag from the other's backside,
but she'd never seen it played out on the limbs of a tree before.

"Even with wings, I don't think I'd risk that." Tia shook her
head quickly as she pulled her attention back to the task at hand.
"Right. I've just got to run in and give these to Mom and I'll be
back. You all set?"

"Mmhmm." Even as she murmured her assent, Meela's sharp
eyes never left the dueling duo overhead.

Tia grinned and climbed from the car, grabbing the tote bag
with her mother's files from the back seat. They'd done enough
errands together in the past few months that she was finally

comfortable leaving Meela alone in the car. Meela was good company for the ride, but didn't enjoy going in and out of the public spaces Tia's errands usually brought her to.

She passed a young woman with several books in her arm coming out of the library and held the door open for an older man coming up the walkway behind her. These weren't parents of toddlers — maybe story hour wasn't what had the library bustling this morning? Curiosity made her more attentive as she scanned the lobby and reading room, surprised to find them no more crowded than any other weekday.

Three carousels of large print books lined a large hall leading past the research room on the way to the stairway. Two women stood in the middle of the hall, distracted from their search for a new story.

"She was determined to make a difference. Kiera was originally from down south, you know, and she said a lot of the decisions that are made by the towns up here are made at the county level down there. It's so much more efficient, you see? Instead of ten towns all making ten decisions, it's one decision for the whole county." The woman wore her silver-streaked dark hair pulled back in a low hair-tie, a pair of glasses hanging around her neck on a no-frills black chain.

Catching Kiera's name as she passed, Tia paused and began perusing the last carousel of books, idly pulling out random books and flipping them as though she were reading their blurbs, trying not to look like she was listening to the women.

"That makes sense for some things, I suppose, but can you see Buttonwood Bay residents agreeing to the same sign regulations they have in Jamaica Plain? They allow all kinds of flashy billboards and digital signs in the downtown..." the second woman shuddered, her expression clearly meant to convey how disruptive such signage would be in Buttonwood Bay.

"Ruthie, we're not in the same county as Jamaica Plain, are we? So we wouldn't have to adopt their sign regulations!" The first woman sniffed. "I think she could have made a real difference here. Not that Stuart Hamilton is doing a bad job of it; I just think she would have brought a different perspective to the board."

The conversation turned to the historical committee's latest meeting agenda, which apparently did not include Ruthie's suggestion for a recipe book fundraiser, even though she had made the suggestion in plenty of time to have it on the agenda. Tia realized she was holding a book on taxidermy and hurriedly put it back on the carousel.

Tia took the wide marble stairs to the second floor conference room where her mother's meeting was. Though it was still a couple of minutes before the hour, the room was filled with the buzz of chatter. Tia found her mother sitting at one end of a semi-circle of tables and handed her the tote bag.

"There's a lot of people here!"

"Oh, thank you, Tia! I remember most of this, but it's good to have the papers just in case." Her mother glanced around the room before adding, "There's a few more than I expected, but the Fling is less than two weeks away. We've been planning this for almost a year!" She smiled up at Tia.

A woman at the middle of the center table sat up straight and cleared her throat. The signal traveled like a spark through the room, and the chatter lulled. Tia met her mother's eyes and hitched her head toward the door before making her way back downstairs.

Back in the car, Meela was still watching the tree. Tia started the engine. "All set. Ready to go to the studio?"

Meela nodded. "Did Tia see the Pyskies playing Fighting Flamingos?"

Tia chuckled. "I did. They were very... committed."

As she drove, Tia replayed her conversation with Cookie. The police were narrowing in on Zinnia. Tia remained convinced Zinnia was innocent, but she had to admit she didn't have all the facts, either. She needed to focus. "I need to find out where everyone was," she muttered to herself. That's what they'd decided on, but the more she thought about it, the less confident she felt.

Tia parked in front of the studio and unlocked the front door. Meela padded in softly, her arms overflowing with the cushion and blanket she carried. She made a beeline for the back room. Tia checked her watch. Fifteen minutes before Kit would be there to check the HVAC system. Tia sniffed the air, uneasy. Now that it had been brought to her attention, it did feel a bit stale inside.

Sighing, she shook her head and followed Meela into the workroom. Meela was busily arranging her blanket nest inside The Burrow, humming a soft tune. She turned her beaming face when she heard Tia approaching. "Thank you, Tia."

Tia grinned. "You are happy?"

Meela smiled sweetly, the dimple flashing in her cheek. "Meela is happy."

Still grinning, Tia walked over to the thermostat on the wall. It showed the temperature as 72, but the switch was off. Should she just wait for Kit? Tentatively, she reached out and flipped the switch. There was a dull thud from someplace in the wall above, then a weak stream of air began to emit from the ceiling vent. Tia bobbed her head in satisfaction once, then froze, her head cocked to one side.

Was that a normal noise? There, again! Hastily, she switched the unit off. The tapping that had begun soon settled out. Tia twisted her hands together, uncertain, then stepped away from the thermostat. Kit would be here momentarily. He would know what HVAC systems sounded like.

Tia paced back to the front room, unable to pretend, even to herself, that the shrill, faint screams she'd heard in the wall were normal. She stood against the wall, crossing and uncrossing her arms. If there were mice, or a squirrel somewhere in the ductwork, and they were caught in the fan, or whatever else had started moving when Tia had turned the unit on...she rubbed her face, trying to dispel the thought.

The front door opened, and Kit stepped through. Tia breathed a sigh of relief and hastened to greet him.

"Morning, Tia! Your dad said something was up with your HVAC, didn't think it had enough power." He pushed his cap back and scratched his balding head. "Said you're gonna need something that cleans the air well, with all the painting you'll have going on."

Tia nodded eagerly. "I hadn't even realized there might be a problem, but I just tried to turn it on, and..." She led him back to the workroom with a grimace. "It sounded okay at first, but then I heard...well, I don't know what it was. I shut it off."

Kit set down his toolbox and approached the thermostat, examining it closely. "Alright, let's see what we got." He flipped the switch to 'on.' The dull thud echoed from the wall, followed by the sound of air moving weakly through the vents.

"Hmm," Kit said, peering at the overhead vent. "Ought to have more power than that. Sounds like it's wore out..."

"Wait," Tia interjected, her hand on his arm. "Listen."

They stood in silence, listening to the air conditioner hum. Then, a faint tapping sound came from inside the wall, followed by high-pitched squealing.

Kit's eyebrows shot up. "Well, I'll be. Sounds like you've got some unwanted guests in your ductwork."

He switched the unit off again. "Critters, most likely. Probably got a nest in there. I'll need to take a look at your roof unit and see if I can flush 'em out."

He rummaged in his toolbox, pulling out a screwdriver and a flashlight. "Might be birds, might be squirrels, might even be Pyskies. They like making nests in cozy places." Kit winked at Meela, who was peeking around the corner of the box house.

Meela ducked her head, but Tia saw her dimple flicker into place, and the normally shy Nowbi didn't hurry to hide in her house.

Tia followed Kit as he found the roof access and climbed to check out the unit on the roof. The mesh screen covering the fresh-air intake vent curled out at one corner as though it had been pried up.

Kit bent down, carefully peering inside with his flashlight.

"Yep, there's something in there, all right. Looks like a nest, made out of...oh my, is that yarn?" He chuckled. The beam of the flashlight shifted, momentarily catching on two bright, beady eyes peering back at him.

"Well, hello there." Kit stepped back. "Definitely Pyskies. Looks like the whole family."

Tia stepped forward cautiously, trying to get a glimpse. "Are they okay? Are they hurt?"

"They seem fine," Kit said, "just startled. But that nest is blocking half the airflow. It's gotta go. Don't want your electric bill going through the roof."

"But...what about the Pyskies?" Tia asked, her anxiety bubbling up again. She could imagine the chaos that could ensue with angry, displaced Pyskies. She'd seen what a mischievous bunch they could be.

"They'll be fine," Kit said, a hint of impatience creeping into his voice. "They can build another nest. It's not safe for them to be in here, with the fan and all. Could get seriously hurt."

Before Tia could respond, a chorus of tiny voices erupted from the vent.

"We were here first!"

"This is our home!"

"We're not hurtin' anythin'!"

Tia winced and kneeled down near the vent. "Hello? My name is Tia. We're not trying to hurt you. We just want to make sure you're safe."

"We're safe in here!" one voice retorted.

"But," Tia explained gently, "the air conditioner...it's not really a safe place for a nest."

Another voice, sounding a bit older and wiser, spoke up. "We've been here for weeks, and nothing has happened. We're careful in the nest."

"The building was empty, so the unit wasn't running. The studio is opening next week, though, and the unit will be on. Tell you what," Tia continued, an idea forming in her mind. "What if we find you a new place to live, somewhere that's safe and dry, but not in the HVAC system?"

There was a moment of silence, then a cautious voice piped up. "Like where?"

"Well," Tia said, her gaze drifting around the roof, "I've got some wood, I could make you a shelter and we could put it up here on the roof. It wouldn't have to be far."

Another short silence, then the initial voice came back louder. "Okay, but if this shelter isn't good, we're moving back."

"We'll make it work. I promise." She turned back to Kit. "Do you think you can get the nest out without damaging it?"

Kit lifted an eyebrow in surprise, then grinned. "And they call *me* squirrel corn! Sure, we can get the nest out. Best to get a box for temporary, at least."

Tia nodded and scrambled back to the ground floor. She quickly scanned the room before spying an old wooden soda box. Dumping the drawing supplies onto the counter, she hurried back to the roof.

Kit had already removed the screen covering and stood ready. The Pyskies hovered overhead, close enough to see and shout instructions, but not within reach. Three of the Pyskies seemed almost to hang suspended in the air together. It was a moment before Tia realized that the two on either side were gripping the middle one tightly, their wings fluttering furiously as his hung at an awkward angle.

Kit carefully maneuvered his gloved hands into the vent, slowly and gently lifting the yarn nest. A few twigs and feathers drifted to the rooftop, but overall, the nest held together as he placed it into the side-turned box.

As he stepped back, the Pyskies zoomed in to inspect their nest. A round-faced, middle-aged female zipped out and seized the feathers that had fallen, swiftly returning to the box with her treasures. Their shrill voices were soon bantering between themselves, ignoring the people on the roof.

"Okay," Tia said, clapping her hands together. "Crisis averted! Thank you, Kit. Now, about this HVAC unit..."

***

Kit tinkered with the unit for another hour, replacing a few belts and cleaning out a substantial amount of dust and...other things, from the ductwork. Finally, he wiped his brow and straightened up.

"Well, Tia, I got it running, but I'm not gonna lie, this unit's tired. It ought to get you through the Spring Fling, but I wouldn't count on it lasting much longer than that. You're going to want to let your landlord know what shape this is in. It shouldn't fall on your shoulders to replace it."

Tia grimaced. He was right, but she had a feeling Luke might say her contract suggested otherwise. She wrote Kit a check and walked him to the front door, promising to let him know if she ran into any more problems.

Sighing, she pulled out her phone and sent a quick text to Luke, then went back to the workroom.

"Meela! Oh my goodness, you've been busy!"

Meela turned to smile at Tia from the tabletop where she kneeled, surrounded by paper and cardboard she had sorted into stacks. "Meela likes to help."

Tia gazed around the now tidier space in amazement. Her colored pencils stood in a crock on the desk, her scissors hung neatly on the pegboard, and more of her paints were grouped on shelves according to medium. "Wow, Meela! I don't know what to say! I mean, thank you!"

She pulled out a stool and slumped down next to the table. "There was a family of Pyskies in the vent. I've told them I'll make them a different shelter for the roof."

Meela sat back on the table, considering. "They will like that. Pyskies like to be where they can see things."

Tia nodded. She needed a nap. She glanced at her phone, and astonishment that it was only two o'clock rolled over her in a fresh wave of exhaustion. She groaned. "Meela, I'm going to get a coffee. Do you want me to see if Cookie has anything good to nibble? Do you want anything to drink?"

Meela's eyes widened hopefully. "Meela loves nibbles! And prickly pear juice."

Tia smiled, nodding, and heaved herself back to her feet. "I'll be right back."

Chapter 13

T ia locked the door to the studio and trudged next door to the Gingersnap. These last few nights of not sleeping well were catching up with her. She needed caffeine and Meela deserved a treat. The bells on the door jingled merrily as she stepped inside, momentarily cheering her with their welcoming tinkle.

The warm cinnamon and vanilla scent of the café enveloped her. Nikola, busy wiping down a table near the bookshelves, looked up at the bell's announcement and smiled in greeting. Several older women were settled on the couches in the sitting room, sipping tea and discussing something animatedly.

"Hey, Tia! What'll it be?" Nikola asked cheerfully.

"Hey, Niki. Something with lots of caffeine, please, and a prickly pear juice and...what looks good for nibbling today?" Tia scanned the pastry case, spying some twisted cinnamon churros. "Oh, one of those!"

Nikola smiled sympathetically, ringing up her order. "You've been busy lately! Think you'll be ready to open for the Fling?" She expertly pulled a shot of espresso and set to work steaming milk.

"Well, that's the plan!" Tia stifled a yawn and settled at the end of the counter, close enough to overhear the conversation in the sitting room without actively eavesdropping. They seemed to be debating the merits of various mystery novels.

"...and then, of course, there's the Agatha Christie method. Everyone's a suspect!"

"Oh, but that's just lazy writing," another woman sniffed. "The best mysteries are the ones where the clues are all there, but you don't see it until the end."

One woman shifted in her seat. "Well, I need to go let the dog out. I left early to drive for the COA this morning. Poor thing is probably crossing her legs by now." The acronym snagged Tia's attention, and she turned casually on her stool to see who was speaking.

"Are you still driving people to their appointments, Martha?" The Agatha Christie hater clearly thought Martha was wasting her time.

Her tone was lost on Martha. "Yes, I volunteer a few days a month. Chuck White had an appointment this morning. He had such a terrible headache."

Tia's ears perked up.

"Oh, the VA," a woman on the other end of the couch responded knowingly.

Tia's mind raced. Chuck. The VA. The alibi.

It wasn't a perfect match, but it was something tangible. Tia maneuvered nonchalantly over to the entrance when Martha pushed herself from the couch. She smiled easily and held the door open as Martha approached. "I'm sorry to butt in, but I overheard you talking about Chuck White and the VA. I know him a bit. Did you take him today? I hadn't realized his head was still bothering him."

Martha looked surprised but pleased to chat. "Yes, poor thing. I took him last week, and he was feeling better by the end of the week, so it made that long wait worth it. But the headache returned over the weekend, so back in we went this morning! He's such a nice man, it's a shame he can't get rid of these."

Tia nodded. "Yeah, I heard him Friday say he drank some kind of tea, and it helped get rid of his headache." She forced a small laugh. "He said it took all afternoon to get that advice."

Martha nodded solemnly. "Oh, he was fit to be tied, having to wait all that time!"

Tia groaned. "You didn't end up caught in rush hour traffic, did you?"

Martha's eyes widened as she remembered the trip. "Oh, my heavens, it was like herding snails through syrup! It was after six by the time we got back. If it'd been my appointment, I would have had dinner someplace in the city and skipped the traffic, but you know Chuck — he wanted to make sure his bunnies were okay, so we came straight back. That man takes better care of those animals than he does himself — and don't think I haven't told him so!"

Tia nodded sympathetically. "It's good he has you to help him."

Martha smiled and patted her hand. "It does me as much good as it does him. Now, I've got to go see to my dog!" She strode purposefully down the sidewalk.

Niki waved Meela's prickly pear juice at Tia before setting it next to the wrapped churro on the counter. When Tia stepped back to the counter to collect her order, Niki leaned in and whispered, "what's the verdict?"

Tia grimaced. "Not sure who it was, but it wasn't Chuck. Did you know he has pet rabbits? I didn't expect that one! Still, that's good news, right? I just have to eliminate all but one."

Niki smirked. "How many do you have left?"

Tia wrinkled her nose. "The rest of the town?" She shook her head. "Not really. Maybe three or four. Hey, did Cookie go home? I thought she was working this afternoon."

Niki shook her head. "She was working this afternoon, but she had to run out for something. She said she'll call if she won't be back in time to close up."

Thanking Niki and paying for her drinks, Tia headed back to the studio.

"Meela?" Tia set the drinks and churro on the table and surveyed the room. When she didn't immediately see her, Tia walked to the box house and peeked inside.

Meela sat silently wrapped in her blanket, peeking through the window facing the back door.

"Meela?" Tia's pulse picked up speed at her tiny friend's demeanor, but she kept her voice soft and gentle. "What's wrong?"

Meela finally turned her large eyes to meet Tia's gaze. "The man with the wide smile but tangled roots went on the roof. Now the man is in the alley."

Tia's gaze flew to the roof hatch. It was ajar. She faced Meela again. "Someone is up there? Who? How did he get in?"

Meela shook her head helplessly. "The man was up, but now is down. In the alley. The man has been here before. The man has keys."

Tia rocked back on her heels. "Luke?" He was the only man she could think of that Meela would know had been there before, other than Kit. And Meela had seemed to like Kit. Plus, Luke did have a key. She was pretty sure he wasn't allowed to enter the premises without letting her know, though.

Frowning, she headed for the roof.

***

Tia pushed the roof hatch open further. She didn't see anything amiss from when she and Kit finished with the HVAC repairs. Even the pyskies were surprisingly quiet. Tia squinted at the box Kit had placed their nest in, but couldn't detect movement.

A scraping sound from the alley drew her to the edge of the roof. Luke was kneeling on the pavement where the corner of the studio almost touched the flower shop. What was he doing? She held her breath as she inched closer to the cornice, her stomach fluttering uncomfortably. Why weren't their railings up here?

As though he felt her gaze, Luke turned his face up and scanned the rooftop, calling out as he spotted her, "Tia! Come, quickly! You need to see this!"

Frowning, Tia returned to the roof hatch. What could he possibly want her to see? Was there something connected to her HVAC system located at that corner of the building? She climbed back down the ladder and headed out to the alley.

"What is it?"

Luke held up a small, stained piece of paper. "I was checking on your HVAC unit, following up on your text. I did a quick scan of the roof while I was up there, doing due diligence, and decided I'd better take a look at it from below, as well. I found this piece of paper snagged against the building." He turned confused eyes on her. "It's a request for a meeting, on letterhead from The Green Thumb." He thrust the paper toward Tia. "There's something on it — it looks like blood!"

Tia cautiously took the paper. A dark, smeared stain marred the corner. It was a request for a meeting, as he'd stated, but it wasn't addressed to anyone. She turned confused eyes back to Luke's face.

Luke ran a hand through his hair. The cuff of his shirt sleeve slid back, exposing his wrist, and Tia's gaze rested on the thin, almost healed scratch there. He dropped his arm and braced his hands on his hips. "The police are looking at the woman who runs that shop. This looks like she was trying to hide this here."

Staring at the paper in her grasp, Tia's brain feverishly tried to put this puzzle piece into the mix with the rest of what she'd learned.

"The police need to see this. They can test it and see if that's blood." He ran his hand through his hair again, looking wildly around the alley. His eyes returned to Tia. "You should call them."

Disbelief surged through Tia. "What? Why do I need to call them — you're the one that found it!"

Luke tilted his head slowly, his eyes narrowed. "Well, you don't have to be the one to call. I thought you might prefer to, given where it was found. If you don't take this to the police it might look like you were hiding it. But if you call them now, it shows you're being transparent."

When Tia didn't immediately agree, Luke drew a deep breath in through his nose and closed his eyes as though he was in pain. "My girlfriend, Jessica, just died over this mess. I spent hours at the station yesterday, trying to help the police go through their evidence and find some answers. Now, here's a potential clue to this murder, and you don't seem to want to bring it to the attention of the police?" He pulled himself stiffly to his full height as stared down at her coldly.

Despite standing in the full sun of the afternoon, Tia suddenly felt a chill. "I don't have a problem bringing it to the attention of the police." She pulled out her cell phone and dialed the station. "I want to get to the bottom of this as much as anyone, and I have nothing to hide. But I didn't find this, so they're going to want to talk to you."

Tia reported the discovery to the dispatcher and assured him they would wait for the detective to arrive, then ended the call. "He said we should wait inside and not touch anything else out here."

Luke nodded silently and followed her back into the workroom.

Tia's gaze fell on the worktable as she strode away from the door, eager to put some distance between herself and Luke. The newsprint pad was open to the list she and Cookie had been brainstorming that morning. *Fairy spit! Had Luke seen that?*

Tia quickly grabbed some other papers and stacked them on top, then moved the whole pile to a shelf as though she was simply tidying the space. She picked up her coffee and Meela's juice and churro and moved them to the desk, risking a nonchalant peek into *the Burrow* to see how Meela was doing. The only part of the Nowbi visible was the end of her fluffy tail, protruding from under the blanket.

The sharp rapping at the front door announced Detective Montgomery's arrival. Tia unlocked the door to let him in and led him back to where Luke remained. He surveyed the room, his gaze scanning every corner and shelf. "Ms. Jenkins, Mr. Garcia. I understand we have another development."

Tia nodded, twisting her fingers together before catching herself and stopping. "Luke said he found this in the alley." She gestured to the stained letter lying on the worktable.

Luke stepped forward, his voice smooth and controlled. "I was here checking on the HVAC unit after Tia texted that she had a problem with it. I decided to do a survey of the building from the ground level, and found that snagged against the corner of the building. There's something on it — it looks like blood. It's from the florist shop. I'm sure Tia's not involved in helping the Kromera woman, given she's a person of interest, but..." He trailed off, shrugging, an expression of concern etched on his face.

Detective Montgomery's eyes narrowed, darting between Luke and Tia. "Why don't you show me just where you found it?" His suggestion was an order.

Luke nodded decisively and led the way. "It was right here, stuck to the side of the building." He pointed to the corner.

Detective Montgomery scanned the alley and the buildings slowly before motioning them both back inside. He pulled out a small evidence bag and carefully slipped the letter inside. "What time were you here with Kit, Tia?"

"Between twelve and one-thirty," Tia responded promptly. She shot a quick glance at Luke. "I went to get coffee around two, and when I came back, Luke was in the alley."

"And you were here alone?" He turned back to Luke, his expression unreadable.

"Yes. I came by to make sure the handyman had done the job right, and no, I didn't see anyone else around."

Detective Montgomery wrote in his notepad. "Alright. Thank you both for your time. I'll be in touch." He gave Tia a pointed look. "Let the police handle this from here, Tia."

Tia bristled silently as the detective left.

Luke lingered.

"Tia, I'm sorry about this," he said, his voice low. "I just... I want to find out who did this to Jessica. I know you do too."

Tia sighed. "I'm sorry for what happened to Jessica. I hadn't realized the two of you were dating. I just can't believe Zinnia Rosewood was involved."

Luke grimaced. "Well, I'm sure the police will pursue the evidence, wherever it leads."

Tia schooled her face into a sympathetic expression as she ushered him out the door and locked it behind him, then turned and hurried to the workroom and her cooling cup of coffee.

Chapter 14

Tia took a sip of coffee and grimaced. *Blech*. Coffee should be piping hot or frosty cold, but never this barely warm mouthful of tepidness. She eyed the prickly pear juice and crouched near the Burrow, considering the Meela-shaped bump in the middle of the blanket.

"They're gone, Meela. Just you and me here."

A moment of silence passed before a soft rustling disclosed the Nowbi's movements. She poked her head out from under the blanket, her twitching ears alert to every corner of the room, before sitting up and dislodging the blanket altogether. Her eyes sought Tia's briefly before staring at her lap.

Tia's shoulders slumped as she studied her friend. Kindness clung to Meela like moss to a rock, but Tia was never sure how to help when her gentle soul got overwhelmed with life's tension.

"Are you ready for a sweets break?"

Meela's head lifted, her eyes large and hopeful. Tia laughed and walked back to the table. "Here you go." She set the juice and churro down before pulling the newsprint pad back over to the table.

Meela's lips curved softly as she scrambled from the box house. "Tia is generous to Meela." She settled on a stool next to the table and delicately began nibbling the pastry.

"That's because you make my life so much better!"

Tia dropped onto the next stool and opened the pad to the list. Chuck was officially off the list, so she grabbed a marker and wrote in Martha's name and "after six" under Chuck's name, drawing a firm line underneath. That left Stuart, Jessica . . . was Luke somehow involved? Zinnia, and...Holly? Was she really considering Zinnia? It still seemed impossible to her.

Meela leaned against Tia's side, hugging her biceps. "Tia is sad?"

Tia sighed and rubbed a hand over Meela's clasped hands. "More frustrated and overwhelmed, but maybe a little sad. The police are still looking at Zinnia for this murder, but I'm trying to figure out who else could have done it."

She pointed to the individual names on the list as she explained. "The woman, Kiera, had an argument with Stuart Hamilton about Chuck White that afternoon at the Gingersnap. She had her nails done at the salon, and then later she was seen storming back to the salon when only Jessica was there. Then her body was found behind the flower shop dumpster, and the murder weapon — which was from the salon — was *in* the dumpster."

Meela followed the explanation with solemn eyes. She carefully popped the last bite of churro into her mouth and dusted the cinnamon sugar from her fingertips.

Tia took another sip from her coffee cup and shuddered. "I can't. This coffee is beyond me." She smiled at Meela. "Are you ready to go home? I've got to get some caffeine in me, but if you want to go home I can make a cup there."

Meela nodded. She hopped down from the stool and followed Tia to the front door. "Does Tia know why someone wanted the woman to die?"

Tia held the door open for Meela and locked it behind them. "No, I don't know."

As she climbed behind the wheel, Tia considered Meela's question. "It's almost like a Wampus chasing its tail -- if I knew who, I'd know why, and if I knew why, I'd know who. Unfortunately, I don't know either."

Meela nodded, her eyes searching the sky through the windshield. "Tia should find someone who saw. Then Tia would know."

A laugh burst from Tia's lips. *If only it could be that easy!* "Yeah, Meela, I need to find someone who saw."

***

Meela scurried past Tia into the house, disappearing around the corner as the door was still swinging closed. Tia knew she would take a careful survey of every room, meticulously observing anything that might have changed in the time she had been away.

Tia strode straight to the kitchen and readied her coffee. The press of a button and a few minutes of sorely tried patience, and she had her reward. She added sugar and a splash of cream before lifting the cup to her lips, hesitating as she inhaled the rich aroma. The first sip was pure bliss — hot, strong, and exactly what she needed. As she cradled the mug in her hands, she mulled over the list in her mind, each name a question mark.

The sound of the door to the garage opening brought Tia back to her surroundings. Her mother's steps stopped in her office before she made her way to the kitchen.

"Thanks again, Tia, for bringing those papers to the library. People can be very good at remembering what's been suggested, not necessarily who said they'd be responsible for doing it." She filled a glass with water from the door of the fridge and took a long sip. "But this is really going to be a great celebration. We're going to have face painting, and wandering minstrels, and old-fashioned skills games on the lawn of the Town House.

Brews Brothers is going to do a cider garden, and Mad Duke Diner is planning a dinner theater of some sort — he told us about it, but I didn't get all the details because I've got enough other things to keep track of. I'm sure it'll be fun. Oh, and we've got Toad and Company again. They're going to be the opening band this year because Nicky's got a wedding at the Silver Dream Resort that night."

Tia grinned at her mother's animation. The more enthusiastic her mother got, the wilder her hands moved as she spoke, gesturing and adding emphasis with abandon. "Better watch your water!"

In response, her mother downed the remaining water in the glass and stuck out her tongue at Tia. "How was your afternoon? Did you get everything done you wanted to?"

Tia gave her a quick rundown of Kit's visit and the follow up of Luke finding the letter in the alley. "I have more to do, but I brought Meela home and needed coffee."

Her mother eyed the cup Tia still cradled. "If you're having trouble sleeping, coffee at this time of day isn't going to help. Why don't you take a break? Have some supper before you go back."

Tia heaved a sigh. "What are we having?"

Her mother smiled, crinkles appearing at the corners of her eyes. "If I call in the order, will you pick up the pizzas? I really don't want to cook tonight!"

The lure of melted cheese smothering warm red sauce on crispy crust was too great. "Ooh, I'll have pineapple on mine. Thanks!"

Agreeing to grab the soda, Tia grabbed her keys and headed back out. There were five pizza shops in town, but the Jenkins' always got theirs at A Pizza The Action. The afternoon was cooling off, making Tia glad she wore a sweatshirt. She decided to try for a parking spot near the store rather than the town lot.

She spied an opening a block away and pulled in. Grabbing her purse, she was out of the car and headed down the sidewalk before she spotted Stuart Hamilton sitting on a bench with a woman just ahead. His arm draped on the back of the bench and his fingers traced circles on her shoulder.

Tia tried for a casual smile. "Stuart? Hi! I didn't expect to see you here."

Stuart looked up, a flicker of surprise crossing his face before he composed himself. "Tia. Good afternoon. This is my wife, Elizabeth." To his wife, he said, "Tia is opening an art studio uptown."

Elizabeth Hamilton, a woman with kind eyes and a gentle smile, nodded to Tia.

"Nice to meet you." Tia could feel her face heating. "Got chilly all of a sudden, didn't it?" She paused, returning her attention to Stuart, then plunged in. "I'm actually in a bit of a...situation. I know I told you I found Kiera's body. I've been trying to reconstruct her day."

Stuart's face tightened slightly, but he motioned for Tia to sit on the other end of the bench. "I don't know what I can tell you, Tia."

"I know you argued with her at the Gingersnap that day," Tia pressed gently. "Could you tell me what that was about?"

Stuart sighed. "It was nothing that matters anymore, really. She accosted me, said I was using town resources to help a man in town because he is a buddy of mine. It got rather heated. I told her I wasn't using town resources, but I was helping a good man out. She said I was breaking the law by doing it." He glanced at his wife, an apologetic look on his face.

"And...were you?" Tia asked, pushing the point.

He looked back at Tia, disappointment in his eyes. "I wasn't breaking any laws, but I was helping a friend. He is very private. Going through all the 'right channels,'" Stuart used his fingers to form air quotes, "would have humiliated him. I just lined up the help he needed."

Tia chewed on the inside of her cheek. She already knew, but still, she had to ask. "Was your friend Chuck White?"

Stuart hesitated, his gaze scanning the nearby area. He leaned closer to Tia and lowered his voice. "That's between me and him, Tia. The man has a right to his privacy."

Tia nodded slowly, respecting his reticence, but also feeling stymied. "Did you see Kiera again that day?"

"After the Gingersnap? No. I had things to do at Town Hall, and then later I had..." he paused, glancing at Elizabeth, "well, later I went to see my friend. I wanted to let him know about Kiera's accusation, in case she decided to make it public. I didn't want him to be blindsided."

"What time was that?" Tia asked, her mind racing.

"It was mid-afternoon, maybe around three? I went to his place, but he wasn't home. I left a note asking him to call me when he got in. Then I went home and took the dog for a walk."

"Did he call?"

"Yes, just as I was heading to the selectmen's meeting. I wound up being late to the meeting, and we found out during the meeting that her body had been found." He leaned forward, forearms on his knees, frowning. "The thing is, Kiera was sharp. She wanted rules applied evenly, to everyone. There was a lot about her to respect. But she had little empathy, and she couldn't see the difference between guidelines put in place for efficiency and actual laws. She thought she was doing the right thing; she was just trying to be a cleaver instead of a paring knife."

Elizabeth tucked her hand in Stuart's arm, and he straightened, putting his hand over hers. He met Tia's gaze, his eyes searching. "I hope this helps you to get past this."

Tia forced a smile. "It does. Thank you." To Elizabeth, she added, "I'm sorry for interrupting your evening. Thank you."

Rising from the bench, Tia gave a final nod and headed toward the pizza shop. The conversation with Stuart provided some context, but the 'why' remained infuriatingly elusive. Was there any way for her to verify Stuart's story?

She pushed open the door to A Pizza The Action, the familiar aroma of warm garlic and oregano washing over her. She gave her name at the counter and grabbed a bottle of soda from the cooler, paying for the order while the pizzas finished cooking.

Leaning against the wall while she waited, Tia pulled out her phone and found the town's website. She checked the calendar; there had been a selectmen's meeting scheduled at seven that night. She clicked through to see the agenda and found a link to the local cable station's recording of the meeting. Her eyes sharpened as she studied the screen.

The meeting started with Stuart apologizing for the late start of the meeting, saying he'd been unavoidably detained. Tia sped up the replay, then had to rewind a bit when she saw a police officer cross the room. He handed a note to Stuart, who read it and paled before abruptly closing the meeting.

Hmm. So that much had been true.

The Hamiltons were gone by the time she stepped back onto the sidewalk. The warmth from the boxes radiated through the cardboard as she carried them back to the car. She carefully placed the boxes on the seat and hit the seat warmer button before heading for home.

***

"Pizza's here!"

Tia carried the stack of pizza boxes to the kitchen table where her parents and Meela were already waiting. Her dad was setting out napkins, and her mother reached for the bottle of soda to fill the glasses she'd set out. Meela climbed onto a stool, eyes bright with anticipation.

The next few minutes were filled with sounds of satisfaction as they bit into slices of pie. Tia recounted how Kit had found the Pyskie nest and fixed the unit, and noted Kit's insistence that it wasn't her responsibility to pay for a new one. Then, she moved on to Luke's unexpected visit to the studio.

"He said he was inspecting the unit and found a letter on Green Thumb letterhead," Tia said, picking a piece of pineapple off her pizza and popping it into her mouth. "He kind of insinuated if I didn't call the police, I was trying to hide evidence. I thought the whole thing was kind of strange, how he just showed up, and then his behavior in the alley, but maybe it's how he's processing his grief."

Her father grunted in response.

Her mother, however, was more vocal. "The Green Thumb? I've been using them for years, and I've never seen any letterhead. They always give me a generic office supply receipt."

Tia paused, pizza halfway to her mouth. "Really?"

"Absolutely. I keep all my receipts for when we do taxes. It's always the same nondescript page, nothing fancy. She's got a rubber stamp of the shop name, she must stamp the entire book at one time. Even when I've contracted with her for parties, there's never been official stationery."

Tia's energy returned even though it seemed improbable. She looked at her parents, then back at Meela, her thoughts churning, a chaotic blend of gathered facts, possible alibis, lingering suspicions, and unproven claims. "So where did this letter that Luke had come from..."

"Seems like he was pretty determined for the police to see it as evidence." Her father finished his glass of soda and rose to pour some more. He stood for a moment with his back to the table, as though debating with himself. "There's something about that man I've always steered clear of, though I can't put my finger on it."

Meela, engrossed as she had been in polishing off her pizza, nodded quietly. "The man smiles wide but has tangled roots."

Tia paused, staring at Meela. "You said that earlier! Meela, what does that mean?"

Meela's round eyes focused on Tia's face, a small frown playing across her lips as she searched for a different way to express herself. "The man...moves like wind through empty hollows." At Tia's continued confusion, she added, "The man hides the sting in the honey."

Understanding washed over Tia. "You're saying he's deceptive! You don't trust him!"

Meela nodded, her shoulders relaxing with relief at having made her thoughts clear. She reached for another slice of pizza.

Tia thought for a moment. "Right. I didn't like him being at the studio when I was out. I'm not even sure that's legal, but even that aside, I think I'm going to get some cameras for inside the studio. Nothing expensive, but I'd feel better knowing if someone is in there without me."

Chapter 15

Tia carefully tacked a tiny shingle onto the pitched roof of the miniature house, holding the tiny brad steady with a pair of beading pliers so she could tap it in with her hammer. Meela crouched on the worktable with a paintbrush, carefully putting little dots of color on the boards Tia planned to use to represent window boxes.

"Tia is sure dots look like flowers?"

It was the third time Meela had asked, and Tia smothered a smile. "I'm sure, Meela. Here, take a look at this." She pulled out her phone and found some pictures of pointillistic paintings. "See how your brain makes it into a vase of flowers, or, in this one, a whole field of flowers? These paintings are all just dots!"

Meela's nose twitched suspiciously, but she nodded and went back to adding dots of color to the trim pieces.

"Almost done!" Tia announced a few minutes later, turning the house for Meela to admire. "Just need to let the paint dry, and then we can add the finishing touches."

Meela put the paintbrush in the jar of water and studied the house. "Pyskies will love Tia's house." She paused, tipping her head thoughtfully. "Would Tia make the Pyskies a basin, too?"

Tia's eyes lit up. "That's a great idea, Meela. I saw a "No Pyskies!" sign near the birdbath at the Brews Brothers the other day. The Pyskies were still splashing about there, but they might like somewhere else to go." Thinking of the layout of the roof made her pause. "I think I'll have to put it in the alley, though. I don't want to bring water up the ladder."

Meela smiled, the dimple in her cheek making its quick appearance. "Meela can watch Pyskies in the alley!"

Tia laughed softly before turning her attention to the bag she'd dropped on the desk when they'd arrived. She'd already set up the new Wi-Fi for the studio. Now she used the paint-drying time to get the cameras set up.

Meela peered curiously at Tia's phone as Tia set up the app for the cameras and checked to make sure she wasn't leaving any blind spots. She secured one to the wall of the studio facing the front door, as well as one above her desk facing the rear exit, and a third that would catch any activity near the roof hatch. She'd purchased a set with four cameras, but three seemed to cover everything.

"Tia will watch her phone when she is not in her studio?"

"Oh, no, Meela. At least, not all the time. This has a way to set it up so that it sends me an alert if it senses movement, see?" Tia made a few changes to the settings and then walked into the front room and returned. The phone's chime coincided with her exit of the studio.

Meela bent over the phone. "Tia is walking — no, Tia is leaving her studio."

Tia smiled at Meela, then scrutinized the phone. "It looks like there's about a ten second delay in the reporting." She furrowed her brow, thinking through the implications. "I mean, I don't honestly expect to need this as security. It's not like I keep valuables here — I literally recycle trash! This just gives me back-up if I ever need it. See here?" She thumbed to another setting. "I have it uploading to the cloud. It'll keep the recordings for a month, in case I ever need to go back and look."

Meela's eyes lifted to the ceiling as though expecting to see a cloud, but her gaze caught on the roof hatch and diverted her attention. "Does Tia think her paint is dry?"

Tia grinned. "I bet it is! Let me add your window boxes, and we can bring it up!"

Excitement brightened Meela's eyes, and she clasped her hands under her chin as she crouched to watch Tia secure the dot-arrayed trim boards under the windows. Despite the exterior appearance of the farmhouse, the interior was similar to the Burrow — one large space. Tia wasn't sure if the Pyskies would utilize storage besides their nest, so she'd created cubbies where the eaves of a traditional house would be.

"Ready?"

To her surprise, Meela dropped her eyes to the floor and shook her head. She swallowed before mumbling, "Meela will wait for Tia to come back."

Tia stared at Meela, then the house, then the roof hatch, and finally back to Meela. She touched Meela's shoulder gently with one finger. "Do you not like heights, Meela?"

Meela shook her head ever so slightly. Her shoulders were hitched and her ears lay flattened to her head. Tia frowned, unsure of what to say. She didn't know much about her Nowbi friend's life before she came to live with her parents, but she'd never seen this kind of reaction from her.

She kept her voice light and gentle. "It's okay, Meela. I'll be right back."

Tia carried the house awkwardly up the ladder, struggling for a moment to get the hatch open. She glanced back at the table and was unsurprised to see Meela disappearing into the Burrow.

Carefully gripping the wooden house in one hand, Tia climbed onto the roof. Once there, she set the shelter down, ensuring it was secure against the HVAC housing. Three Pyskies edged to the opening of the wooden crate Tia had brought up the day before, cautiously peeking around the side at this new offering.

"Look! The new home I promised!" Tia called out, gesturing for them to come closer. "What do you think?

The Pyskies exchanged glances, skepticism warring with curiosity.

"Hmph! Maybe she's not all rustle, no root?"

"Tha's a big 'un, Jassie!"

"What — now we gotta make the nest over ag'in?"

Their words were directed at each other, muttered from the sides of their mouths while trying to appear casually unimpressed to Tia. She chewed her bottom lip a moment, unsure how to proceed. She hadn't thought about what a big job it would be for them to move their nest.

"Uh, I could move your nest in, if you like it," she offered.

One of the larger males sauntered boldly toward the house, eyes darting back and forth between Tia and the front door he was aiming for. Tia took a slow step back, and he froze, quivering slightly with distrust.

"Why don't you check it out, see if it meets your needs?" She gestured over her shoulder with her thumb. "I'll wait over here, give you some space."

She took a few more steps away and sat, crossed legged, near the hatch.

After a moment of silence, another Pyskie fluttered over to the house, its arms crossed over its chest. When Tia didn't move, the third scampered to join the first on the porch. Another half-minute ticked by before their curiosity overcame their suspicion and they were inside the house.

The inspection didn't take long.

The first Pyskie glanced up at the house with a hint of begrudging admiration. "This isn't half bad, I suppose. Top notch, even."

Tia's heart lightened at his compliment, but she stayed where she was until the three had returned to the wooden crate. "Will it do? Do you want me to move your nest in?"

Their longing to claim the new house was obvious in their expressions, even from this distance. She couldn't hear their murmured conversation as she moved closer, but their darting glances and hesitant peeks into the crate caused her to remember the Pyskie with the injured wing yesterday.

"I will be very careful. I can lift the whole thing at once and move it in — look! I made it so the roof can unlatch..." Tia crouched and unhooked the little catch she'd installed, swinging the roof up on its hinges.

The larger male took a deep breath before coming closer. "Tawny...he's still in the nest. You can move him, too?"

Tia swallowed furtively, uncertain. She wasn't sure she wanted to pick a Pyskie up..."Yes, of course I can." She nodded firmly. "I'll be very careful."

It took no time at all. The nest resembled a large ball of fluff and yarn with occasional twigs and feathers poking out, with a mouth at one end. Giving herself no time to second guess her offer, Tia carefully scooped the nest in both hands and gently tucked it into the new house. She swung the roof back down and refastened it.

As she turned her gaze toward the little assembly, she noticed a few feathers had fallen. She picked them up and held them out in a flat hand.

"Will Tawny be okay?" She had to ask.

"He'll get better!" The big male's chest puffed up with bravado.

"You should'a seen us!" another Pyskie piped up, eyes gleaming with the thrill of recounting. "We wen' up ag'in the Ashmouth man!"

Tia tilted her head, her curiosity roused. "The Ashmouth man?"

"Yep! He speaks such lies, his tongue must be coated in ash!" There was a gleeful edge to his inflection. "We threw mudballs and dung bombs at his car! He 'as yellin' an' shakin his fist—"

"And Tawny, oh Tawny, he flew too close!" the third chimed in, his voice chilled. "Ashmouth grabbed him. Hurt Tawny, he did, but we didn't let up! We attacked until he threw Tawny away—but we showed him! We snatched his shiny right off his wrist!"

"Oh, my!" Tia knew her wide-eyed reaction delighted the Pyskies. Their wings buzzed with excitement, their cheeks flushed with the remembered action. "Listen, I've got to get going. I was thinking, though...would you like a..." she caught herself before naming it a birdbath, "um, a basin? I could put one in the alley near the studio's back door, where I could refill the water easily?"

"A splashin' basin? Woo hooo!"

"Yeah! Take that, Brewsies!"

"Would it be safe? Ashmouth sometimes hides things in the alley. 'Member, Jassie? 'Member that body?"

Tia straightened abruptly, speaking too eagerly as she caught the comment. "Did you see someone hide a body in the alley?"

The pyskies shot upward, startled by the sudden change in Tia's energy. The air around them glittered with potential explosive current. At least they didn't send any charges zinging her way.

"I'm sorry! I didn't mean to startle you!"

The pyskies hovered overhead only briefly before zooming away. Tia followed their flight into the branches of the Buttonwood trees in the town parking lot. Sighing in frustration, she headed back downstairs.

Cinderberries!

If she didn't care about breaking the trust she'd begun building with them, she'd badger Tawny for answers. Tawny couldn't fly away...but she'd seen angry pyskies before. In a good mood, they were mischievous and could be pesky, but get them angry, and they could take their pranks to a whole other level.

***

Tia stepped down from the ladder, her heart still encouraged with the Pyskies' bubbling enthusiasm for the house. She glanced around the studio for Meela, her eyes quickly landing on the Burrow.

"Meela? They loved it! And you were right, I think they liked the idea of a basin to splash in!" Tia called gently. "I'm not sure, but I think they also might have seen what happened the day of the murder."

After a moment, Meela's face poked out from beneath the blanket in the middle of the burrow. "Tia will make the basin? Tia will put the basin in the alley?"

"Yes! They seemed to love the idea, although they said sometimes the Ashmouth man hides things like bodies in the alley."

Meela blinked, the slight curve of her lips hinting at her satisfaction. "Tia found someone who saw!"

Tia offered a ghost of a smile. *Yeah, I found someone who saw, but I don't know anyone named Ashmouth. Or anyone else who would consider anything pyskies said worth listening to.*

"Meela could help? Meela could help Tia make the basin?"

"Absolutely!" Tia nodded enthusiastically. "I was thinking we could use some of the garden materials from the house. We've got pots and stones—perfect for a little Pyskie oasis! What do you think?"

Meela clambered out of the Burrow, and Tia felt a rush of warmth at her friend's returning confidence.

As Tia swung her purse over her shoulder, keys in hand, her phone chimed. It was her mother.

"Tia! I don't suppose you're heading home before dinner, are you? Would you mind swinging by the grocery store on your way home? I wanted to make salad, but the lettuce has gone bad."

Tia rolled her eyes, glad her mother couldn't see. "We were actually just leaving to come home. I'll stop on the way."

Tia looked over at Meela, who was already waiting to climb into Tia's car. "Meela, I just need to stop at the store first. Mom says the lettuce is bad and she's making salad for supper. Then we'll work on the basin."

Meela nodded and settled in for the ride.

Tia pulled into the grocery store parking lot, her mind still humming from her encounter with the Pyskies. The sky was overcast, and the air had the scent of impending rain. Tia lowered the windows a couple of inches before shutting the car off. "I'll be quick," she assured Meela before heading into the store.

Inside, she headed straight for the produce section. Her hand reached for a bag of mixed salad greens before she realized what she was doing. On her own in Providence, bagged salads were one of the few reasons she went to the produce section. Here?

Mom would be appalled!

Laughing softly at her near-blunder, she scanned the produce display. Spying the heads of lettuce, she grabbed two, then added an orange bell pepper from the adjacent shelf.

Turning to head toward the checkout, she spotted Holly and Zinnia Rosewood at the end of the aisle, their basket nearly filled.

"Hey, you two!" Tia called out and quickened her pace to reach them. Zinnia looked tired, but managed a warm smile. Holly stood slightly behind Zinni, her expression subdued as she fiddled with the hem of her shirt.

"Hi, Tia! How are you?" Zinnia's voice was hoarse.

Tia searched Zinnia's face. "Worried about you guys, actually. I heard you were away for the weekend."

Zinnia's gaze flickered with a hint of sorrow. "Yeah, we've had quite a lot on our plate lately." She glanced sideways at Holly, who simply nodded, though her tight-lipped expression betrayed her unease.

"Is everything's okay?"

With a deep breath, Zinnia shared, "Holly's mother went missing a few weeks ago; that's when she came to find Jacob. We've been trying to figure out what happened to her mom. This weekend, we were following up on some leads the private investigator turned up."

"Missing? Oh, that's awful, Holly," Tia said, her voice laced with empathy. "I'm so sorry." She paused, searching for the right words. "I can't imagine... is there anything I can do to help?"

Holly shook her head, forcing a brief smile. "Thanks, Tia. There really isn't anything anyone can do."

Tia nodded, a lump forming in her throat. She wanted to offer more, but she sensed Holly's reserve. Feeling clumsy and inadequate, she abruptly remembered the scene with Luke and the paper he'd found on her roof. The invitation to a meeting...

A wave of reluctance washed over her. She hated to add to Zinnia's burdens. But the police had the paper, and she knew Detective Montgomery would follow up on it.

"Zinnia," Tia began hesitantly, "there's something else... I was having work done on the HVAC unit and texted Luke Garcia about it. Luke came to check on things and found a page of the Green Thumb stationery in the alley. He said there was something that looked like blood on it." She winced. "I'm so sorry, but he insisted we call the police about it. I just didn't want them to come asking you about it and for you to wonder why I didn't say anything."

Zinnia's face paled slightly, but she remained composed. "Stationery? I don't have any stationery for the Green Thumb."

Tia frowned, her mind racing. "My mom said she didn't think you did, that you have a stamp you use on your receipts. This definitely had letterhead that said the Green Thumb, though."

Zinnia sighed, her shoulders slumping slightly. "This just keeps getting worse and worse, doesn't it? But you know," she added, straightening her shoulders and looking Tia directly in the eye, "I trust that the police are smart enough to realize when evidence is being manipulated. Someone is trying to make me look guilty, but I didn't do anything."

Tia shook her head emphatically. "I believe you, Zinnia! I know you couldn't have done this!" She hesitated, adding, "I'm here if you need anything, okay? Really, anything at all."

Zinnia gave Tia's hand a grateful squeeze. "Thank you, Tia. That means a lot. We've got to get going. We're just getting back from the weekend, we've got no food in the house."

Tia managed a smile and nodded before getting into line at the checkout. The bagger tried to make small talk about the upcoming Spring Fling, but Tia barely registered his words, her mind still replaying her conversation with Zinnia. She paid for her items, grabbed the bags, and hurried back out to the car.

Meela perked up when Tia returned, her eyes bright with anticipation. "Tia is back!"

"Yup! Lettuce acquired." Tia tossed the bags into the backseat. "Let's go home. I've got some things to figure out."

Chapter 16

T ia topped off her tumbler with hot coffee and snapped the cover on, nearly overturning the cup as she put her breakfast bowl and spoon in the dishwasher. The fact that the Spring Fling was in three days and she still had boxes and bags of supplies all over the studio workroom had woken her in a panic this morning, giving speed to her movements, if not grace. She quickly wiped up the rest of the evidence of her breakfast from the counter, put the yogurt back in the fridge, and almost threw the strawberry tops in the trash.

Forcing herself to pause and count to ten even as she gritted her teeth, Tia picked up the strawberry bits where they'd fallen on the floor and tossed them into the bin.

You can't do any more than you can do. But if you hurt yourself, you could do less, she reminded herself.

One bite at a time.

Rolling her eyes, Tia grabbed her coffee and phone and headed for her purse. Time with Cookie would help right now, but she hadn't really talked to Cookie since Monday. After their brainstorming session had been cut short by Tia needing to get the papers for her mum, Cookie went to work. But when Tia stopped in later, Nikola said Cookie had run out for something.

Tia had texted Cookie a couple of times since then, but she wasn't even sure Cookie had seen the messages. Not like Cookie at all. A knot tightened in Tia's stomach. She quickly typed another message:

Hey, you okay? Haven't heard from you. I miss you!

A beat. Then another. Still no response.

Finally, Tia grabbed her keys and headed for her car. Maybe immersing herself in Spring Fling preparations would distract her. She wanted to create a display showcasing her upcycled crafts. It could attract more clients, or maybe even open up new supply avenues. At the very least, it would offer topics for conversation.

As she reached for the door handle, her phone buzzed. It was Cookie. Relief washed over Tia, quickly followed by concern as she read the message:

Hey! So sorry, Luv! Total chaos!! My cousin was in a car accident out of town, and I had to rush over and help my aunt. Watching my younger cousins, ferrying them to soccer, library, clubs — I'm exhausted! Wasn't trying to ghost you!

Tia blew out a breath she hadn't realized she was holding. "Chaos" described Cookie's life on any given day, even without a family emergency. Tia quickly typed back.

Oh, Cookie, I'm so sorry! Of course, family first. Everything okay with your cousin? And your aunt? She hesitated, then added: **When you get a sec, can I call? I could use a Cookie-boost, but only if you have time.**

Tia waited, her fingers drumming against the cool metal of the car door. The silence stretched, punctuated only by the chirping of birds in the overgrown hedge that lined her front yard. Maybe Cookie was already back on kid duty.

Suddenly, her phone buzzed in her hand.

"Tia! I've missed you! Ugh, poor Jellybean got banged up pretty good but she's going to be okay. I mean, considering the alternative; she's lucky to be alive! Her friend who was driving is still in ICU. The car they were riding in is definitely totaled. Aunt Tutti is frazzled, but she's holding it together. She wanted to stay with Jellybean at the hospital, though, and Uncle Tim had to work, so I've been keeping the kids under control." Cookie finally took a breath. Her voice was just as energetic as ever, but pitched low and suspiciously quiet.

"Why do you sound so muffled? What's going on? Are you hiding or something?"

Cookie snickered softly. "Because I've only got about ten more minutes before I have to wake the munchkins up and get them ready for school, so of course I'm hiding! Aunt Tutti said she can bring Jellybean home today, so she'll be able to get the rug rats off the bus this afternoon. Which is good, because I love these guys to the moon and back, but I've got a cafe to run!" She sighed. "So that's me — what's going on with you? Have you learned anything new about the murders?"

"Cookie, I woke up this morning and realized the Spring Fling is in three days and I am so under-prepared! I'm on my way to the studio now to make a display of projects I've completed, but there's so much to do! I'm not sure how many people to prepare for, either, so now I'm second guessing the project I've planned..."

"Tia, that's why it's called a soft-launch, hon! But if it would make you feel better, maybe have a couple of activities planned. Not to offer everything to everyone, but if you do the one you planned and you run out of supplies, or it doesn't go as you thought, you just switch to another one. It's no biggie! Some shops just have a table on the sidewalk with free candies and sale items! I bet you could put out chalk and section off squares on the street for people to draw in and most people would love it!"

Tia's eyebrows lifted in surprise. "That's actually a really great idea!"

"Don't sound so surprised, it happens!" Cookie laughed, then groaned. "Oh, cinderberries, they're up! Tia, I gotta go, but I'll be back this morning."

Promising to stop in at the Gingersnap, Tia rang off, grinning. Her heart was always lighter after a chat with Cookie.

***

Tia pulled up into the alley behind the studio. The memory of finding Kiera's body still had her glancing at all the doors and windows and into all the shadows before shutting off the car. She parked, popped the trunk, and winced at the sight of the overflowing boxes and bags. Three days until the Spring Fling. With the amount she still had to do, it felt more like three hours.

"Right, then." Shaking her head with a renewed sense of determination, she started unloading, the muscles in her arms already protesting with each heavy box of broken pottery, pieces of metal, and various types of paper she used. This was the last of her supplies from Evie's room,

A couple hours later, sweat trickled down her back, plastering her t-shirt to her skin. The studio was starting to resemble something other than a storage unit, though. The large front room was clear, and most of the art supplies were in the back workroom. Some of the projects she had completed over the last few months were displayed on the shelves her mother had donated. Though the Burrow remained in the workroom to give Meela a safe space, miniature houses and fairy homes constructed from recycled paper and glass bottles sat prominently in the windows, where they could invoke the interest of passers-by.

As she sorted through a disheveled stack of newsprint pads, the one she'd been most recently using caught her eye. Tia turned to the suspect list she and Cookie had compiled. The more time has passed, the more certain she was that Luke had definitely seen it before Detective Montgomery arrived.

Picking it up, she ran a finger across the scribbled names and phrases. Chuck White, she'd crossed off already, adding his alibi to help her keep things straight. Now she slid onto a stool and did the same for Stuart Hamilton, noting the meeting he was at, and Zinnia and Holly. She bit her bottom lip as she jotted down their whereabouts the day Kiera was killed, and the weekend.

What a way to find out you've got a kid!

Sighing, Tia's eyes fell on Jessica's name. Could she have done it and really committed suicide? It just didn't feel right. Jessica had seemed nervous talking about Kiera's visit, but.... What motive would she have had? Tia thought about the names on the envelope she'd found. The envelope Luke had taken from the studio.

Hadn't he? It had to have been him.

Tia tapped the end of the pencil on the pad. She was positive Luke had taken the envelope; she just wished she had proof. She glanced around the workroom and sighed, shoulders slumping. Time to finish putting away the last of the supplies. Pushing away from the table, she stood and stretched, arching her back until she felt it pop. She hefted a large box of plastic lids from various juice and water bottles and scanned the shelves for an empty spot.

After what felt like hours, the last supply was stowed, the last cardboard box flattened and stacked with all the others. She surveyed the workroom, taking an inventory of where she still needed better organization. She had thought she had plenty of built-ins now, but now she wondered if she'd have time to add more pegboard against the far wall for more flexible storage.

A rumble in her stomach reminded her she hadn't eaten since her rushed breakfast. Glancing at her watch, she realized she'd been at it for hours, completely losing track of time. She envisioned a juicy burger; the Brews Brothers' Tavern across the street was calling her name. Throwing her purse over her shoulder, Tia locked up the studio and headed out, anticipation spurring her across the street.

Tia strode up the walkway, glancing at the empty birdbath. There was no water inside, and a few more "No Pyskies!" signs announced their messages from the nearest lamp posts. Inside, she slid onto an empty stool at the bar.

"A burger and a soda, please, Barry." Tia smiled up at the bartender, a man whose smile seemed permanently etched on his face.

As she waited, she idly scanned the dining room. Luke Garcia was there, seated at a table with Cheyenne from the salon, and another woman whose shirt prominently displayed the salon's logo. They were wrapping up their conversation, gathering their purses and nodding solemnly at Luke's imploring expression. Cheyenne dabbed at her eyes before the two women headed for the door.

Barry set her soda down, the ice clinking merrily in the glass. "Got chilly again, didn't it?" he asked, nodding towards the streets. "That's New England, I suppose. Weather's supposed to warm up this weekend, though. Be great if we could figure out a way to keep the jangle witted pyskies out of the birdbaths! Patrons don't love getting soaked by the little twitch-wings, especially when it's cool!"

Tia nodded, swirling the ice with her straw. "I'm opening a studio across the street, and I've been trying to get everything ready for the Spring Fling. I've been working for hours, but it's finally shaping up."

Barry cocked his head at her. "A studio, huh? That's different." His eyes focused past Tia and he lifted his chin in acknowledgment. "Good luck to you," he offered before moving off to the man signaling him from the other end of the bar.

Tia's phone chimed, indicating a text. Tia swiped her thumb idly to unlock the screen, resting her elbow on the bar. Cookie's message made her groan. Poor Cookie couldn't catch a break!

One of her younger cousins had woken up with a stomachache, and now most of the family, Cookie included, was taking turns in the bathroom and carrying bowls around in case they couldn't make it. Tia tapped in a commiserating text and sent it on its way before glancing around the room again.

Luke had moved to another table, near enough that Tia could almost but not quite hear what he was saying. He spoke animatedly to a woman with short, dark hair tied into place with a silk scarf, his hands moving expressively as he talked. His voice was just a murmur, though, so Tia couldn't make out the words. He took the woman's hand and squeezed it before he spoke to another person, this time stopping at a corner that made him audible to the bar.

"... something we can all do together -- a way to remember Jessica. A candlelit vigil, maybe, down by the gazebo. We'll be gathering around seven. People need to grieve, to come together. I just... I just can't believe she's gone," he finished, his voice cracking with emotion.

Luke paused, pressing his fingertips to his temples for a moment before he was on the move again, patting shoulders and murmuring what Tia assumed were invitations to his vigil as he made his way toward the door. He paused by a table of elderly women, his head bent in earnest conversation, before finally exiting the tavern with a final, lingering look of grief.

Tia watched him go, a knot of disquiet sitting uneasily in her stomach. A candlelit vigil? A public display of mourning? Was this genuine grief, or was Luke playing a role? She took a long sip of her soda, the sweetness doing little to dispel the bitter taste in her mouth.

Just then, Barry set her burger down, the aroma of grilled meat and melted cheese filling the air. "Here you go!" His smile was as friendly as ever. "Enjoy."

Tia smiled in thanks and took a bite, the hot, savory flavors momentarily distracting her. But as she chewed, her mind continued to churn. The contractors' names on the envelope. Jessica Rivers, dead. A Green Thumb letterhead found in the alley. Luke Garcia, orchestrating a vigil. It sure felt like everything was connected, but how? And what role did Luke play in it all?

Chapter 17

Tia arrived back at the studio, the remnants of her burger still dancing on her taste buds. The knot of unease hadn't completely dissipated, though. Luke's performance, as she now thought of it, still bothered her. She pushed it aside, focusing instead on the task at hand: the Pyskie splash basin. In the alley, the Pyskies could splash to their hearts' content without soaking any patrons.

She found the large, sturdy terracotta dish she'd brought from the house, along with a collection of smooth, colorful stones and a stack of empty plant pots. Lastly, she grabbed one of the empty cardboard boxes from her morning haul.

The space behind the studio was barely big enough for the dumpster and her car, but Tia envisioned a small section at the corner of her building becoming a pyskie paradise. She stacked and glued the pots together with exterior adhesive, carefully balancing the dish on top.

Satisfied with her handiwork, Tia stepped back to admire her work. It was simple, but she knew the pyskies would love it. She added the bag of stones to add extra weight to make sure the adhesive secured the dish, then carefully upended the cardboard box over the top. She didn't want the pyskies to find it before it was dried, safe, and ready to be used.

"What's this?"

The squeaky voice came from just behind her. Tia whirled, her heart beating a little quicker even as her eyes quickly located the hovering pyskie.

"Hey! You startled me!" She fanned her chest, exaggerating her reaction at the pyskie's obvious glee. Smothering a smile, she gestured over her shoulder at the basin. "Remember I told you I would make a splash basin for you guys? Once this is all dry, I'll uncover it and add the water."

The pyskie's wings sped even faster, and his mouth dropped open. "You did it? For real?" He flew in a tight circle. "Wait here!"

He shot upward, leaving her standing, open-mouthed. *What?*

In less than a minute, he was back, along with one of his friends.

"See, Jassie? She done it!" He gestured at the box. "'S under that!"

Tia's lips twitched with the effort of containing her amusement. Trust them to uncover her surprise before she was ready!

"It is, but it's not ready yet. It has to have time for the glue to dry before I put the water in and you can use it." She allowed herself to smile. "I'd say tomorrow morning, okay?"

The two dropped to the ground at the base of the sculpture, peering up into the underside of the box. The second pyskie, who must be Jassie, jutted his chin forward as he considered the structure. Nodding once, he flew back over the edge of the roof without a word to Tia.

"Is there something wrong with it?" Tia wondered aloud.

"Oh, no, missus! Jassie liked it!" The first pyskie was aloft again, hovering a few feet in front of Tia.

His hair was blond and stuck out in tufts around his head. Now that she looked at him closely, Tia was surprised to note he looked cleaner than she expected. Well, except his . . . breeches? She wouldn't really call them pants, nor shorts...whatever they were, they were the color of dirt. Tia suspected it was because they were largely covered with it.

Realizing she was staring, she blurted, "What is your -- " She caught herself, swallowing her words. Just in case there was any truth to the old lore about not asking magical species their names, she carefully rephrased her question. "I've heard you call him Jassie, and there's one called Tawny; what do they call you?"

He grinned knowingly, a twinkle in his eyes. "Oh, ho! She knows! She doesn't ask for names!" He giggled as he turned a somersault in the air before continuing, "But you can call me Masin."

The buzz of wings near her head caught her attention, and she ducked quickly, covering her face with her arm. Her spasmodic movement sent Masin into convulsions of laughter, and Jassie, who had flown back down from the roof to address her, shot several feet away before recognizing that she wasn't trying to catch him.

"Sorry! I didn't know you were right there." Tia tried to reassure him as she lowered her arm and straightened up.

Jassie kept a wary eye on her as he kept his distance, hovering above the overturned box and dropping something on top of it. Masin, catching his breath as his laughter finally subsided, explained.

"It's the Ashmouth man's shiny! We nicked it from him when he grabbed Tawny! A gift for a gift, see? For Wick-mender." His eyes still glowed, but the wicked gleam was gone.

Tia understood that this gift, both the shiny and the name, was a big deal. "Thank you."

She reached out and plucked the shiny object from where it had landed on the box. It was a man's bracelet, crafted from thick links of sterling silver. The clasp was undone, and closer examination revealed the delicate hinge was snapped in half, most likely a sign of its forced removal. She turned it over in her hand, the cool metal heavy in her palm.

"Thank you again. I promise I'll add water to the basin first thing tomorrow."

Masin and Jassie exchanged an exuberant glance before zipping back up to the roof. Tia watched them go, her mind already racing through the implications of their gift. Who was the "Ashmouth man"? And what did being "Wick-mender" mean for her?

Her phone rang, snagging her attention. It was her mother.

"I know you were out early this morning and you're probably exhausted, but I was with Jamie's mother and she said Jamie has a bunch of sonotubes heading for the dump this afternoon, and I thought those might be something you could use? I didn't want to tell her we'll take them without you looking at them, though."

Tia's eyes flared, her interest flaring instantly. "Absolutely! Where are they? Let me lock up here and I'll come now!"

***

"So, then he dropped this silver bracelet on the box!" Tia laughed, scrubbing at a stubborn bit of burned something on the bottom of the casserole dish. "They called the man they took it from 'Ashmouth,' which...one of them said it's because of the lies he speaks. I don't know, but they seemed awful proud of bringing it to me. And, I think they called me 'Wick-mender,' which I also don't understand."

Meela slid the plates in the dishwasher, carefully arranging the plates by size in the rack. "The pyskies like Tia."

"I think they might," Tia agreed, rinsing the dish and placing it on the counter above the dishwasher. "Also, if I'm right, I think this Ashmouth man is the one who hid Kiera's body. I just don't know how to figure out who it is."

"Tia will think of something!" Meela chirped, closing the dishwasher and starting the cycle. "Will Tia watch her cameras tonight?"

Tia glanced at Meela, her brow furrowed in contemplation. "I hadn't thought about it. I suppose I could, but I don't really expect anything to happen."

Meela fidgeted, her tail flicking from side to side. "Meela could watch. Meela can tell Tia what she sees."

Tia's eyes softened as she gazed down at her friend. Meela must still be upset about Luke letting himself into the studio.

"I'll tell you what, Meela. I can set up the camera feeds on my laptop if you'd like. You don't have to watch it; I bought the cameras for back-up. But if you want to, you can watch to your heart's content."

Meela's large eyes met Tia's, and she nodded. "Tia can do it now?"

Tia allowed herself a small chuckle. "Sure, Meela, I can do it now."

Her laptop was in the living room. She opened it and quickly pulled up the browser window. Pointing to the trackpad, she showed Meela how to wake the laptop if the camera feed wasn't on the screen when she wanted to watch, and reminded her which screen was from which camera.

Her gaze fell on the white rectangle laying cockeyed on her worktable — her list of suspects and clues. She twisted her lips, furrowing her brow. There had to be more to the story than she knew. If Jessica had really killed Kiera, and then printed her note before . . . a sudden idea struck Tia.

"If Jessica didn't have a printer, she would have had to print that note elsewhere. Where would she do that? She'd want to keep it private, right?" She bit her bottom lip, staring unseeing at the laptop screen. In her mind's eye, she saw Jessica checking her reflection in the window before going into Luke's office. She refocused her attention on Meela, who was intently scanning the screen . . . because of Luke's intrusion... Tia's gaze flicked to the clock on the wall; almost seven.

"Meela, I'm going to go check something. I need to see Luke's office. I'll be back in a bit."

A frown flickered on Meela's face, but she said nothing as Tia grabbed her purse and ran for the car.

Tia chewed on her lip as she sped toward the town parking lot, her mind racing. She briefly considered calling Cookie, but remembered what her friend was dealing with and shook her head. Better not to add to Cookie's plate at the moment. Besides, Tia didn't want Cookie to worry. If she shared her plans, Cookie would worry, and feel responsible if Tia got caught.

The parking lot was nearly empty; most of the shops were closed. Tia wondered how many people were down at the wharf for the memorial. She pulled into a space, killed the engine, and sat for a moment, scanning the street.

What am I doing? This is crazy!

She took a deep breath and got out of the car, pulling the hood of her sweatshirt up against the evening chill. The storefronts were dark and quiet, the workers already gone for the night. Across the street, the Garcia Family Real Estate office had a faint glow of light coming from a back room, but the room on the other side of the large front window was dark.

Tia crossed the street and tried the handle. It was locked, as she expected. She jiggled it a few times, watching and listening to see if anyone moved around where the light was on. Nothing.

She moved to the corner of the building, checked the street for any passersby, then ducked into the narrow alley between the real estate office and the consignment shop next door. Heading for the back of the building, she tested each window as she went. The last window, aglow with warm light, gave under her hand.

It wasn't latched.

Tia's pulse quickened. Glancing toward the street one more time, she pushed the window up a few more inches, then squeezed through, her heart hammering against her ribs.

The room was an office break area with a small kitchenette. It smelled of burned microwave popcorn, and Tia guessed the reason for the open window. She closed the window as quietly as possible, then stood still, listening. The only sound was a low hum from the refrigerator. She edged cautiously into the hallway.

The walls were painted a sterile beige and lined with framed photographs. Tia paused to look at them, her eyes scanning the smiling faces. Here was Luke, shaking hands with beaming homeowners in front of freshly sold houses. Luke with a family holding keys, their faces radiating gratitude. Luke at a community event, accepting an award. Tia leaned close, examining one of Luke with his arm around the shoulder of an older man, both in front of a restaurant near the wharf.

A silver chain glinted around Luke's wrist.

Tia scanned the hall quickly before reaching up and pulling the picture from the wall. She couldn't be sure, and she sure wasn't coming back here later to check.

Next, she turned her attention to the large printer at the end of the hall. It was a large office machine, the kind of slick color copier/printers that would be able to print marketing brochures as well as the documents a property sale would require. A box sat on the floor just beside the printer, half-filled with discarded pages. Tia squatted and rifled through the sheets, already knowing Jessica wouldn't have left any mistakenly printed copies of a suicide note.

Half-way through the pile, she found a sheet of letterhead. It was red, not green, and said it was from The Red Door Motel somewhere in North Carolina, but Tia recognized the design of it instantly. Luke must have used this design to create that letterhead from The Green Thumb he supposedly found in Tia's alley.

A quiet tick sounded somewhere behind her. Tia froze, muscles rigid as she crouched on the floor. A heartbeat passed, then another. Slowly, she forced herself to release the tension and turn to assess the area. Relief flooded her belly at the sight of an empty hallway. It must have just been the building.

Hands trembling, Tia folded the paper and shoved it into her pocket.

She continued down the hall, passing two open office doors. The first room had a large conference table and half a dozen chairs. The other had a desk with a couple of chairs set in front of it, an assortment of folders stacked on the desk, and a short bookshelf hosting a few framed photos of a beautiful woman with various other people, including one with Luke. From their similarities, Tia guessed the woman was his mother.

***

Luke's office was the last one on the right. Tia paused at the doorway, her heart doing a little flutter-kick. The room was growing darker as the sky outside did, but enough light spilled from the hallway to see. She glanced at the window and ducked lower, realizing she might be visible from outside.

Crouching, she moved inside, her head swiveling back and forth as she scanned the room. Luke's desk was neat, almost obsessively so. No stray papers or empty coffee cups, like on his mother's desk.

Beside the desk sat a small metal trash basket. Tia grabbed it and used two fingers to pinch an old coffee cup out of the way.

The basket held a couple of crumpled napkins, a discarded sugar packet, and... two envelopes. One was a regular white envelope, the second was one of those business envelopes with a cut out where the address printed on the letter inside would show through. Luke's name was scrawled across the front of each. Tia pulled them out, but they were both empty. She shrugged and dropped the envelopes back into the trash.

The desk drawers weren't locked. The top one held pens, paper clips, and a stapler. A second held neatly organized files in a hanging rack. The third, a stack of file folders. Tia checked one; empty. Her stomach tightened with urgency. This was getting her nowhere.

Her gaze landed on a long credenza against the wall. She moved to it, her fingers hovering over the smooth surface. The top drawer was locked, but the second one wasn't. She hesitated for a moment, her conscience twinging, but pulled it open.

Inside were more envelopes, at least half a dozen, each with Luke's name across the front. Some were printed neatly, others scrawled in disjointed script. Tia picked one up, feeling its weight. Definitely not empty. She opened the first one. A stack of twenties. She fanned them out — there was $100 there. The next one, the same. She opened a third. This one seemed a little thicker. Inside, there was a folded piece of paper along with the cash.

Tia unfolded it carefully, holding her breath. A handwritten note on a scrap of paper torn from a larger sheet read: "Luke, thanks again for the opportunity. I really needed this. If you need any more done, even at a higher percentage, keep me in mind." No signature.

A higher percentage?

Frowning, Tia pulled out her phone, snapped a quick photo of the note, then carefully refolded it and tucked it back into the envelope. She put the envelopes back in the drawer exactly as she found them and closed it, glancing again at the window.

She gasped, fear gluing her in position.

Fairy spit!

Luke stepped down off the curb onto the street, aiming for his office.

Stupid, stupid, stupid!

Tia's brain kicked into gear, and she bent double to get below the window opening. She scrambled for the door and flew back down the hall to the break room. Had she left anything exposed? Had she closed all the drawers? She saw the picture she had taken from the wall laying on the floor next to the box of discarded paper and overshot the doorway to grab it. As she dashed back to the break room, she heard the lock of the front door turning.

Heart pounding and hands shaking, she shoved the window open. A chime sounded as the front door opened. Tia clambered through, wincing as her foot scraped loudly over the sill.

"Hello?" Luke's voice was sharp as he called out from the front of the office.

Tia's trembling made tugging the window closed more difficult. As soon as she jerked it down, she sprinted for the back alley and around the corner. Blood pounded in her ears as she raced past the next couple of buildings, frantically searching for escape. She spotted a footpath into the gas station and took it, slowing to a jog as she neared the pumps.

Her heart battered her ribs. She felt jumpy, nerves stretched taut as a guy wire, but she forced herself to slow further and walk to the sidewalk. Her body screamed at her to go straight to her car and home to safety. Her brain told her to stop at the studio and grab the bracelet first.

Chapter 18

Tia nervously checked the street in both directions, then craned her neck to see if anyone was in the gas station lot. Satisfied she was alone, she set off at a brisk pace, making a wide circle around the block to the back door of the studio. She needed to be certain Luke didn't see her enter the studio. The sound of a car door being closed somewhere in the night made her even more jumpy, but she didn't run into anyone.

Her hands shook as she fumbled with the key in the lock. Finally, the key turned and she slipped inside, bolting the door behind her. The air in the studio was cool and still, a stark contrast to the frantic energy thrumming through her veins. She flipped on the lights, the sudden brightness making her flinch. The workroom looked clean and fresh - a blank canvas, everything in its place. Releasing some of her tension along with a deep breath, Tia headed for her desk.

She'd put the chain in the cup holding her pens before leaving this afternoon. She just needed to compare it to the one on Luke's wrist in the picture.

"Looking for something?"

Tia whirled around, her heart leaping into her throat. Luke stepped in from the darkness of the studio, an intensity to his expression that sent Tia's pulse back into overdrive.

"Luke! What are you doing here?" she squeaked, her voice a little too high. She forced a shaky laugh. "You scared the living daylights out of me."

He didn't smile. "I could ask you the same question. What are *you* doing here so late?"

Tia's eyes skipped around the room, her mind racing. "I had this flash of inspiration -- a sculpture idea wouldn't leave me alone, so... I had to come work on it." She gestured vaguely toward a pile of cardboard against the far wall.

He didn't look convinced. "Now?"

"Creativity doesn't keep business hours!" She tried for an upbeat, flippant tone. "But, listen, Luke. I'm pretty sure landlords have to give notice before just... showing up, right? There are laws about tenant rights. This is the second time you've let yourself in without even notifying me." She took a step back, reaching behind her for the desk. She tried to project casual indifference as she slid the picture she'd grabbed onto the desk and covered it with papers, hiding the incriminating evidence.

He advanced another step, his smile bright without reaching his eyes. "I saw your car in the lot, but your light wasn't on. I just wanted to make sure you were okay."

"Oh, I'm fine," Tia insisted, forcing another smile. "Bursting with innovation, actually. I can't wait to get started." She hoped she sounded convincing. "Please, don't let me keep you. I know you must be busy."

Luke didn't move. "Go ahead, then. Create. Let me watch."

Tia's skin prickled. This felt wrong. So very wrong.

She turned toward her supplies, trying to appear absorbed in her work. "I don't usually work in front of people," she mumbled. She grabbed a fresh pad of paper and a pencil and began sketching out a whimsical mushroom house similar to one she'd already made using clay based around a glass jar. Risking a glance, she saw Luke slowly circling the room, his gaze sweeping over the stacks of salvaged materials, the collection of tools, the half-finished projects.

"You know," he said, stopping near a shelf filled with cans of spray paint. "It would've been so much better if you'd just stuck to your art." He picked up a can of neon pink spray paint, turning it over in his hands. "Instead of... trying to solve murders."

Tia's heart hammered against her ribs. He knew. He knew she was investigating.

But how much did he know?

"Solve murders? Luke, what are you talking about?" She carefully injected a note of confusion into her voice.

"The police have it all sorted out, Tia. Jessica's suicide note explains everything. Why can't you just let it go?" He tossed the can of paint up and down in his hand, his brow furrowed.

"Because some things don't add up, Luke." Tia moved away from the drawing table, placing it between them. "Jessica confessed, yes. But she didn't have a printer."

Luke shrugged, tossing the paint can onto the shelf with a clatter. "Maybe she borrowed one. What does that have to do with you?"

"And the Green Thumb letterhead? It's funny, because my mom shops at Zinnia's all the time. She said the Green Thumb doesn't use letterhead, they use a rubber stamp on their receipts." She let the statement hang in the air, watching Luke's reaction.

His expression flickered, a barest hint of unease crossing his features before his salesman's smile snapped back into place. "So? Maybe Zinnia finally decided to get some. What's your point, Tia? You think she forged it herself?" He chuckled, the sound forced. "That's absurd. She seems barely able to run the shop."

"I think someone wanted to make sure the police suspected Zinnia," Tia countered, working hard to keep her voice from trembling. "Otherwise, why would the letter be so conveniently planted right by the dumpster where Kiera was found?"

Luke's smile faltered. "That kind of thing happens all the time in cases like this."

"Maybe," Tia said, her voice dripping with sarcasm. "Or maybe someone wanted Zinnia to take the fall." She circled the table, putting more distance between them. Reaching into her pocket, she pulled out her phone. "All right, you know I've been doing some digging." She unlocked the screen, navigating to the photos she'd taken in his office. "These are interesting, don't you think?" She held up the phone so he could see the picture of the envelopes stuffed with cash, and the letter asking for more jobs even at a higher percentage.

Luke's eyes widened, his face paling and his lips tightening before he ground out, "So, that's what you were after! I knew you were in my office!"

Tia swallowed. She knew she was treading dangerously, but couldn't help pushing. "Garcia Family Real Estate seems like a thriving business. Are those 'finder's fees' reflected in your quarterly reports?"

He took a step forward, his voice hardening. "That's none of your business, Tia. I connect contractors with property owners. It's a service."

"Kickbacks are illegal!" she challenged. She dropped the hand holding her phone to her side, pressing the phone icon surreptitiously. "Kiera D'Eath was asking about permits, wasn't she? About contractors greasing palms? You were afraid she was going to expose you."

"Kiera was always digging," Luke said, a sneer twisting his lips. "She thought she was some kind of crusader, cleaning up Buttonwood Bay."

"She must have confronted you. Did that make you angry? Was it in front of people? Is that why?" Tia tossed question after question to keep him distracted, pressing her phone screen where she hoped her emergency contact numbers were. It was a shot in the dark, but she knew she wouldn't be able to outrun him, even if she managed to get to the door first.

"She came charging in when she saw me at Sophie's." Luke's glare grew fierce as he remembered. "She stood there waving her list around, insisting she had everything figured out and was going to the Commission. I tried to reason with her, but I admit we got heated."

"And you killed her there?" Tia tried to keep the horror from her voice.

He shook his head. "No, I didn't kill her!" He raked his hand through his hair, the movement of his cuff exposing the still healing cut on his wrist. There was no chain.

"She tripped. Took a step backward and twisted her ankle or something. She was grabbing at the air and she hit that ridiculous sculpture; brought it down on her head." His voice was disturbingly flat. "It was an accident, I swear. I didn't mean for it to happen."

"An accident that conveniently silenced her forever." Tia didn't bother trying to hide her horror anymore. "And Jessica? Was that an accident, too?"

When he didn't answer right away, Tia pushed. "No, she wasn't an accident, because you had to have printed that note. You planned what happened to her before you ever did it!"

Luke's eyes flashed. "Jessica was a mess. I was trying to protect her. I moved the body while Jess cleaned up the blood. But she got scared; she was starting to panic. I told her it would be okay, that I would take care of everything. But... she wouldn't listen."

Tia swallowed hard, her throat dry. "So you 'took care of' her, too?"

He didn't answer, but the silence spoke volumes.

Luke's face hardened, the last vestiges of his salesman's charm disappearing. "Enough talk." He circled around behind Tia and grabbed her arm. Tia subtly placed the phone on the stool, hoping to obscure it from view.

Luke noticed the movement immediately. His eyes narrowed. "What are you hiding?"

He moved faster than she anticipated, his hand darting out and snatching the phone. His glare became thunderous as he saw the active call screen. Before Tia could react, he jabbed the end call button. "That was a mistake." His voice was cold and hard as he tossed the phone onto the desk.

He tugged her to her feet. "Let's go." He dragged her toward the far corner of the workroom. "Up!" He gave her a shove toward the ladder.

Tia dug in her heels, resisting. "Why?"

"I want you to see something." His grip on her arm tightened, the pressure making her wince.

"What?" Her mind raced, trying to buy time, to find an opening. "I don't want to see."

"You will." He punctuated the statement with another, more forceful shove. "Now climb. Unless you want me to help you." The threat in his tone was unmistakable.

Tia started to climb, her hands clammy on the cold metal rungs. She focused on each step, trying to ignore the tremor of fear that ran through her. He was going to push her. He was going to make it look like another accident.

She reached the hatch and pushed it open, the night air hitting her face like a slap. Luke was right behind her, crowding her as she pulled herself onto the roof. The stars twinkled above, mocking the terror churning in her stomach. Buttonwood Bay stretched out below, peaceful and oblivious.

"Beautiful view, isn't it?" Luke said, his voice deceptively calm as he stepped onto the roof beside her.

Tia didn't answer. She could feel his presence, a dark menace at her back.

"All that's missing is a letter," she said, trying to keep him talking. "I can't figure out, though; why frame Zinnia?"

"I've been trying to buy that property for months. She wouldn't budge. 'Oh, it's been her dream to run a shop for years, she's built up a following, blah, blah, blah." He spat the words out like they tasted foul. "I'm the only one willing to say it — this place was better before the pixies, half-breeds, and whatever else crawled out of the brush thinking they deserve storefronts."

Tia stared at him, repulsed. "So, you decided to kill two birds with one stone? Get rid of Kiera and Zinnia at the same time?"

"It was... expedient," Luke said, shrugging. "Hiding the body and the stupid statue behind her shop? It was a perfect opportunity."

Tia ground her teeth. His nonchalance was galling. "When did you decide to plant that invitation on the fake letterhead?"

Luke grunted in disgust. "I knew that was a long shot, but they hadn't arrested her. I just needed to nudge them with a final piece of evidence..."

He stepped closer, his eyes glinting in the starlight. "But you, Tia... you're the loose end I didn't see coming. You just wouldn't let it go. You had to keep digging, keep asking questions. Now..." He reached out and grabbed her arm.

Luke roared, more in surprise than in pain, releasing Tia's arm as he swatted at the side of his head. "What the — "

A streak of light zipped past Luke's ear, followed by a furious warble and a fist-sized nut wreathed in sparks.

A chorus of tiny, angry voices filled the air, their tone high-pitched and furious.

"Leave her alone!"

"Get off our roof!"

"Ashmouth!"

Luke stumbled back, shielding his face with his arms as the makeshift projectiles rained down on him. "Leave off, you sparkrats!" He swatted the air in fury, grasping blindly at the Pyskies flying just beyond his reach.

"Flee, Wick-mender!"

Tia hesitated, but at a second urging to find safety, she scrambled toward the hatch. The Pyskies, their tiny forms darting and weaving through the air, provided a chaotic screen, keeping Luke disoriented.

Reaching the ladder and starting down, Tia's hands trembled so badly she nearly missed a rung. She clung to the ladder, squeezing her eyes shut, while the sound of the Pyskie's battle against the Ashmouth man echoed above her. Tia struggled down the rest of the ladder with her heart in her throat.

She landed unsteadily on the workroom floor and weaved for the door, fumbling with the bolt in her panic. Her fingers slipped on the bolt, her trembling making her whole body clumsy.

Click. It was open.

She threw the door wide just as a fist pounded against it from the other side.

"Police! Open up!" a voice boomed.

Before Tia could speak, a crash echoed from the front of the building. Glass shattered.

"Police! We're coming in!"

Tia stumbled forward. "He's on the roof!" She gestured wildly over her shoulder at the access ladder. "Luke Garcia. He killed Kiera D'Eath and Jessica Rivers!"

Several uniformed officers swarmed the workroom, guns drawn and pointing into corners as they made their way to the ladder. One officer gently guided Tia to the sidewalk in front of the building. "Are you hurt? What happened here?"

"Luke! Luke tried to kill me," Tia said, her voice shaking. "He admitted he killed Kiera D'Eath and Jessica. He was going to push me off the roof. The Pyskies... " She choked back a sob. "They attacked him so I could get away." She was vaguely aware of tears coursing down her cheeks.

***

A stiff blanket smelling faintly of plastic was draped around Tia's shoulders. She huddled into it, unable to stop shivering.

"Tia! Oh, sweetheart!" Her mother's voice cut through the chaos. Tia turned toward the call and found her parents hurrying to her, their faces etched with worry.

"Mom, Dad..." Tia buried her face in her mother's shoulder. Relief washed over her in a dizzying wave. "He tried to... he almost..."

Her father put an arm around both of them, his hands firm and strong on their backs. "Right before you called, Meela called us into the living room to see the camera feed. She'd been watching since you left — she said she knew something was going to happen tonight. We called the police right away."

Her mother smoothed Tia's hair. "Thank goodness you're alright."

Detective Montgomery approached, his eyes narrowed and hair unusually rumpled. "Tia, are you okay?" His gaze scanned from head to toe and back before carefully studied her face, as though he didn't trust her shaky nod. He took a deep breath, his professional demeanor returning. "I hate to do this right now, but I need to take your statement. Can you tell me everything that happened, from the moment you arrived at the studio?"

Tia nodded, steeling her nerves. The relief of being safe, held by her parents, was slowly giving way to the exhaustion and the weight of everything that had happened. She began to recount the evening, starting with her ill-advised search of Luke's office and ending with the Pyskies' unexpected intervention. Her parents listened intently, their faces a mixture of shock, fear, and pride.

Detective Montgomery scribbled furiously, interjecting with questions, clarifying details, and occasionally muttering to himself.

"Okay, Tia," he said, his voice weary but firm. "You've been through a lot. I'll need you to come in tomorrow to sign this statement, but for now, go home. Get some rest." He paused, a hint of exasperation in his voice. "Give the investigation a rest, if only for the night."

"Wait!" She was exhausted, but she had to know. "Are the Pyskies okay? Did he hurt any of them?"

Chapter 19

Tia sipped her coffee, allowing the warmth to seep through her aching body. It had been a terrifying night. Even with Luke in custody, Tia still felt fragile, and welcomed the warmth of Meela's weight as the Nowbi leaned against her arm, her big green eyes tracking Tia's face. "They were amazing, Meela." Tia was still in awe of her little protectors. "The Pyskies were like a buzzing, dive-bombing squadron of defenders."

Meela purred, a low rumble in her chest. "Pyskies hearts sing true. Small wings carry strong courage."

A slow smile blossomed across Tia's face. "They do. They really do." She pictured the scene on the roof, the swarm of tiny creatures attacking Luke, their high-pitched cries echoing in the night. It was almost comical in retrospect, but it had been her only chance.

"I want to do something special for them." Tia said, setting down her mug. "The splash basin will be dry today, and I promised them I would uncover it and add the water, but... they risked their lives for me. A few cups of water just doesn't seem like enough."

Meela tilted her head, her dimple deepening. "Tia could bake sweet nibbles for pyskies' honeyed-hearts."

Tia's eyes lit up. "You're right! Muffins... or cookies! Something warm and delicious — I bet they'd love that!"

Meela nodded emphatically, her tail swishing back and forth. "Sweet crumbs say thank you, make nestmakers happy."

"Yes!" Tia drained her coffee and pushed herself up from the table, a renewed sense of purpose filling her. "Do you want to help me bake some, Meela? We can bring them to the studio later. I've also got to go to the police station and sign a statement, and make sure everything at the studio is set for Saturday."

Meela blinked, her large green eyes lighting with excitement. "Meela may help? Yes!" She ran to the counter and pulled out her stairs, quickly running to the baking cupboard.

A flurry of activity filled the kitchen as Tia gathered ingredients, allowing Meela to mix under a watchful eye. Soon the scent of warm cinnamon, vanilla, and brown sugar intermingled with the lingering aroma of coffee. Before long, a batch of golden-brown cookies, studded with pecans and drizzled with honey icing, were arranged on cooling racks. Tia pulled the last pan from the oven as her phone rang.

She glanced at the screen as she answered, wrinkling her nose at Meela conspiratorially as she put the phone on speaker.

"Hey, Cookie!"

"Tia! Oh my goodness, Luv! Uncle Toffey just told us what happened last night! I can't believe I missed all of this! Are you okay? Did that troll really try to push you off the roof? You have to tell me everything." Cookie's voice was a torrent of concern and excitement. "I'm so glad you're alright. It's bad enough that I wasn't around to help figure this out, but I can't believe we almost lost you!"

Tia laughed, the sound lighter and more genuine than it had been in days. "I'm okay, Cookie. A little shaken, but okay. And don't worry, you'll get all the details. It was pretty dramatic, even for Buttonwood Bay." She grabbed the spatula and lifted the cookies onto the cooling rack with the others.

"Dramatic? Tia, that lunatic is going to be in jail for life, I'm sure! I can't imagine what it must have been like up there with him. I can't wait to actually see you safe and sound. Anyway, I'm headed back into town now. We tracked down the gastronomic miscreant to some macaroni salad Twinkie made. I'm still staying out of the kitchen today per protocol, so Nikola is covering the morning shift and Scott this afternoon. I'll be there by noon, though. I need to see you — to make sure you're okay and give you a giant hug!"

Tia grinned. "I can't wait to see you, Cookie. I have to head to the station soon to sign a statement, and then go check on the studio, but let me know when you're back and we'll meet up."

"I got you, Luv. Just make sure you're not running off solving any more mysteries, ok? I don't need a repeat of last night. I still can't believe that the Pyskies fought him off long enough to save you! It's the best small-town hero story I've ever heard!"

"I promise, no more mysteries for today!" Tia laughed and pushed one of the cooled cookies toward Meela, pilfering another for herself. "Just paperwork, cookies, and maybe a little artistic adventure. See you this afternoon."

She hung up, shaking her head and grinning at Meela. "Cookie's on her way back, and she's already in full Cookie mode." She took a nibble of the golden brown cookie, closing her eyes in delight. "Oh my gosh, Meela, these are incredible!"

***

"So, the silver chain... and the picture you stole. Also, the stationery you thought to put in your pocket. And the cloud access for the studio security cameras." Detective Montgomery consulted his notepad, his expression a mix of irritation and grudging respect. "We'll need all of it, Tia."

Tia winced. "Stole is such a harsh word. I prefer... temporarily borrowed."

"Whatever you want to call it, it's evidence." He sighed, running a hand through his salt-and-pepper hair. "You know, you were lucky. Very lucky. That little stunt you pulled could have gotten you killed."

"I know, I know," Tia mumbled, avoiding his gaze. "But I was right, wasn't I? About Luke, about everything."

"Yes, you were. And that's what makes this so infuriating." He leaned forward, his brown eyes intense. "We were already looking at Garcia. Jessica's confession note didn't add up; once we realized she didn't have a computer or a printer. We had officers looking at Garcia Family Real Estate, planning to bring him in for questioning *today*."

"So you weren't just looking at Zinnia, or me?" Tia felt a mix of relief and foolishness. "You really already suspected Luke?"

"We were pulling all of the threads that might unravel this murder, and there were links between Jessica and the murder," Detective Montgomery clarified. "The nail technician mentioned Jessica was dating him. It was enough to put them both on the radar."

Detective Montgomery scowled. "Look, Tia, I can't fault your intuition. I can't even fault your... well... your risk-taking. You were right, and you helped bring a killer to justice. But you have to understand, what you did was incredibly dangerous. This isn't high school! You could have compromised the entire investigation. Not to mention, you could have been killed! Are you trying to give your poor parents a heart attack?"

"I know." Tia chewed her bottom lip, then blurted, "But I couldn't just sit back and do nothing! Zinnia... she's my friend. And that creep was going to get away with it."

Detective Montgomery leaned back in his chair, the leather creaking softly under his weight. "I understand that. More than you know." He was quiet for another moment, and then he said,

"Tia, you're a good friend. You were when you pulled your fire alarm stunt trying to clear Cookie's name in high school, and apparently that part of you hasn't changed. Just promise me you'll try to be a little less... impetuous in the future, okay? Let us do our jobs."

Tia hesitated. "No promises," she said finally, a sheepish grin spreading across her face. "But I'll try to be more careful."

He snorted. "That's all I ask. Now, get out of here. Go home, get some rest. And Tia?"

"Yeah?"

"Thank you."

***

Tia left the police station, the weight on her shoulders lighter than it had been in days. Luke was in custody, Zinnia was cleared, and the truth was finally out. She still felt a pang of guilt for putting herself in danger, but the relief of knowing she'd helped bring a killer to justice outweighed the fear. Having Detective Montgomery acknowledge the things she'd done was because she was trying to protect her friends, well, that put a cherry on the top of this particular sundae!

Parking in the back alley, Tia grabbed the box of cookies, and then turned her attention to the soon-to-be Pyskie paradise. First, she carefully lifted the cardboard box, revealing the terracotta splash basin now securely attached to the stacked pots. The colorful stones gleamed in the sunlight.

Next, she grabbed a bucket from her studio and filled it with water from the sink, carefully carrying it out and pouring it into the basin. The water shimmered, reflecting the sky above.

Tia stepped back, admiring her work. It was so close, but something was missing. She studied the sculpture. It was bright and whimsical, perfect for Pyskies to play in the sun.... she glanced up at the roof overhang. It was perfect for spring, but once summer came, it might be too hot.

Tia smiled. It could wait until after the Spring Fling, but she was going to rig up an awning to give the Pyskies some shade for their splash basin. Mentally running through the materials she would need to make it reality, Tia grabbed the cookies and headed inside, making her way to the ladder.

She felt a moment of trepidation at how close she'd come to falling from this ladder last night. Closing her eyes, she took a couple of calming breaths to steady herself. She climbed carefully, the box of treats held securely in her hands.

Stepping onto the roof, she was immediately greeted by a flurry of wings. The Pyskies swarmed around her, their tiny voices a cacophony of greetings.

"Wick-mender's returned!"

"Hoppin' jellystars, she's back!"

"Are you okay?"

Tia smiled, her heart swelling with affection for the brave little creatures. "I'm fine, thanks to you. You were amazing last night."

Masin puffed out his chest, his blond tufts sticking up even more than usual. "We showed him, didn't we? Ashmouth didn't know what he was getting into!"

"We threw every burrbriar we had at him! Masin told us, pitch and dive! Pitch and dive! And we did!"

Tia thought this Pyskie might be a female, based on both her slightly softer voice, and the fact she wore something more like a dress than the breeches the males wore.

"Well, then, you deserve a treat." Tia held out the box of cookies. "Meela and I baked these especially for you. They're pecan and honey."

The Pyskies fell silent, their tiny eyes wide with anticipation as they hung suspended, momentarily flabbergasted. Masin spoke, his voice soft for once. "For us?"

"For you," Tia confirmed.

As if a switch had been flipped, the Pyskies descended on the box, grabbing cookies twice the size of their faces and flying off with them. Some devoured them on the spot, crumbs raining down like golden confetti. Others carried them off, perhaps to save for later.

"These are magic!"

"The best crumbels of sweet I's ever et!"

Tia giggled with delight.

Masin flew closer, crumbs dusting his cheek. "Thank you, Wick-mender. You made us happy."

"You're very welcome, Masin." Tia smiled, her heart glowing. "You made *me* happy."

***

Downstairs, Tia had just tossed the cookie box when she heard sharp tapping on the front door, followed by Cookie's voice. "Tia! Open up! I need details, stat!"

Tia burst out laughing as she hurried to let her friend in. As expected, Cookie launched herself into a hug, squeezing Tia tightly.

"Don't *ever* do that again!" Cookie said, her voice muffled against Tia's shoulder. "You scared me half to death."

"I'll try not to be abducted to anymore roofs," Tia promised, patting Cookie's back. "Come on in."

For the next hour, Tia recounted the events of the previous night, with Cookie interjecting with gasps, curses, and the occasional "Oh, Luv, no!" By the time she finished, Cookie looked both exhausted and exhilarated.

"That's toad-smoked," Cookie breathed, shaking her head. "Absolutely toad-smoked! But you did it, Tia! You caught him! And the Pyskies... the Pyskies saved you?! This is the most Buttonwood Bay story ever."

Tia grinned, feeling a surge of affection for her friend and her quirky little town. "I know, right? Who needs superheroes when you have crime-fighting Pyskies?"

Cookie pulled back, her copper waves bouncing. "So, what happens now? Are you all set for the Spring Fling Saturday? How can I help you?"

Tia lifted her eyebrows, twisting her lips in self-deprecating surprise. "You're not going to believe this, but...I think I am ready!"

Chapter 20

T ia adjusted the temporary "Artistic Adventures: Out of the Box Creations" sign she'd hung in the window one more time, blew out a deep, cleansing breath, and unlocked the front door of her studio. Today was the day — the annual Spring Fling, and her softish grand opening!

Out on the sidewalk, tables and booths lined the edge of the streets of the downtown block, which had been closed for this festive occasion. Most of the people bustling about were shopkeepers, but the patrons would descend on them soon.

The air smelled of cinnamon and toasted nuts and...was that warm apple? Tia grinned. Cookie must be baking her apple turnovers in addition to the bear claws, devil's food cupcake bites, and copperseed cruffins she already had in her display cabinet when Tia stopped in earlier.

Cookie had been elbow deep in dough, with so many pastries on cooling racks there was barely room for her mixing bowl. She'd still taken the time to wish Tia luck on her launch, transferring snowsugar onto Tia's shirt when she squeezed her in a hug and pushing a cruffin into her hands before running back to her ovens.

Tia moved a pedestal table onto the sidewalk, thankful for her mother's last-minute suggestion for something to put a few baskets of chalk and a stack of brochures on to attract the residents less likely to walk through her door. She finished arranging her materials and picked up a stick of pink chalk.

Might as well give 'em some inspiration!

Fifteen minutes and three colors later, a large chalked stinglace plant appeared to grow on the side of the studio's entrance. Tia stepped back to appraise the drawing, dusting her chalky hands on the apron she'd donned in an attempt at preserving her clothes.

In the center of the intersection, the sharp rapping of a drum stick launched an explosion of bass and electric guitar. Tia recognized Nick Ford's vocals; Toad and Company were officially kicking off the day's celebration. She hummed along to the rousing tune.

"Tia! Girl, you have such a cute space here!" Tia, beaming, turned at the sound of her name. A blonde woman approached from across the street, a wide smile accompanying her words. She was holding hands with a young girl who was obviously related to her.

The woman looked vaguely familiar to Tia. She kept her smile in place even as she tried to place her.

"Can you believe it's going to be our 15th class reunion this summer? Like, where has the time gone? But look at you — this place looks so great!"

Tia gasped. "Bekah? Bekah Powell?"

Bekah smiled, pleased with Tia's reaction. "Well, it's Bekah Wallace, now. This is my daughter, Rose." Rose's smile at Tia mirrored her mother's. "We saw your flyer for your studio at the Winking Mouse, and Rose really wanted to come check it out! She loves arts and crafts!"

Tia turned her attention to Rose. "That's fantastic — thank you for coming! Do you want to add a picture to my gallery wall?"

She gestured to a basket of chalk and the stinglace plant she'd drawn on the wall.

Rose nodded eagerly. She grabbed the basket and approached the wall. "What should I draw?"

Tia squinted at the wall, considering. "I was thinking of making it into a chalk garden. So, you could add some flowers, or a bird, or something else that you would see in a garden. Unless you had something else in mind!"

Rose shook her head, then turned back to the wall, chalk in hand.

"So, are you married? What have you been up to? I thought you moved away!"

Tia licked her lips and returned her gaze to Bekah. She and Bekah had never been friends in school, but they hadn't been enemies either. Bekah had stayed out of the mean-girl drama.

"Nope, not married! I did move away, but I moved home about six months ago. I've been doing sculptures and upcycled art for a while now. When I saw this space was available, I thought it would be a great way to bring in something the community could enjoy, and at the same time, give myself a little more room for some of my projects."

"What sort of classes will you be offering?" A teenage girl interjected her question, eyes bright with curiosity.

Tia glanced around. More people had approached while she'd been focused on Rose and Bekah. Two more children were adding to the garden mural, and one toddler was alternating making marks on the sidewalk with licking the chalk in her other hand.

"What I do is often called Upcycled Art. I use things most people would send to the dump, and I turn it into sculptures and art projects. I'm going to offer two simple projects today to give people a small taste of what I'm offering. Some classes I'll run will be geared for children, but some," she smiled at the teen, "will be for those with more skill."

The teen lifted one corner of her mouth in acknowledgment at being credited as having more skill than the fledgling artists currently scribbling their way across the studio entrance.

***

The morning flew by, including the sea-creature class Tia hosted just before lunch. She congratulated herself on managing 23 squid projects and the children striving to create them out of toilet paper rolls, poster paint, construction paper, and the shells Tia had collected from Buttonwood Bay's beaches.

Tia labeled the last creature, putting the child's name on a piece of masking tape and adding it to the drying rack with the others. She'd offered parents the option to swing back after lunch to collect the dried projects, and most had agreed gratefully.

She glanced around surreptitiously. Much of the crowd seemed to be diverting to the Brews Brothers' cider garden or stopping at the Gingersnap's tables to buy a sweet and aiming for the church lawn for a short picnic. Dare she grab a few minutes for a breather?

***

Tia slipped out the back door of the studio, breathing a sigh of relief as the noise from the Spring Fling faded slightly. She hadn't realized her studio would draw this much attention! True, some of it was simple curiosity from people who'd heard she played a part in taking Luke down, but a lot of parents and children sounded interested in Tia's classes. It was a good problem to have, but right now, she was knackered and her feet were killing her.

She wandered over to the corner of the building where she'd set up the Pyskie splash basin. Tawny, his injured wing still slightly askew, perched on the edge with his feet in the water. He watched Masin and Jassie frolic in the water, splashing each other with gleeful abandon.

"Having fun, spriglets?" Tia asked, grinning.

"Wick-mender! Jassie is cheating!" Masin complained loudly, eyes shining.

"Are not! You're just cranky 'cause I'm wettin' ya better. Ask the wing-dinger. See?" Jassie paused in his splashing and fluttered above the pool, glancing back and forth between Tia and Tawny.

"Aw, no, don't drag me in! I take no sides!" Tawny shook his head emphatically.

Tia laughed. "Well, it sure looks like you're having fun." She tilted her head and furrowed her brow. "I'm glad it's not too hot today. I need to remember to make that awning. I bet this alley still gets full sun in the summer."

The rumble of a vehicle made Tia turn. Jacob's pickup truck was backing into the alley. Zinnia and Holly jumped down from the cab, pots of lush greenery cradled in their arms.

"Tia!" Zinnia's voice rang with relief and happiness. "I have something for you."

Tia was glad to see Zinnia's eyes were clear and bright, and her hair was its bouncy, brilliant green again. It rivaled the leaves of the vibrant flower growing in the large pot Zinnia carried over to Tia.

"For you, Tia." Zinnia effusively extended the pot toward her. "It's both a thank you and a 'best wishes to your new studio' gift." The flower within the pot was a hybrid double-flowering honeybane Tia had never seen before; several velvety crimson blossoms were edged in white and framed by glossy dark green leaves. The bloom was too rare to have been purchased from a wholesale supplier: Tia knew, without being told, it had to have come from Zinnia's private garden.

"Zinnia, it's beautiful!" Tia took the pot, noticing how the soil was still damp. "Thank you! I really didn't do anything special."

Zinnia beamed. "You didn't give up on me, Tia! Because of your help, I still have my shop. I will reopen on Monday. I didn't want to reopen during the Spring Fling because I didn't want too much attention too soon."

Tia set the plant on the ground and impulsively wrapped Zinnia in a hug. "I am so, so glad."

"I have to bring the rest of these into the shop." Zinnia shifted and her gaze slid past Tia, toward the pyskies still frolicking in the pool. She smiled. "I guess I owe the pyskies my thanks, as well."

Tia grinned. "Careful how loud you say that; they'll be expecting nibbles every day!"

Zinnia leaned closer and whispered conspiratorially. "Right now, I'd happily bring them every day!" She clasped Tia in another quick hug before joining Holly in unloading the truck's cargo.

Tia straightened and took a deep breath before heading back to the fray. The steady stream of people ebbed and flowed, but she could always count on someone being drawn to the chalked mural and the intriguing displays in her window.

"Is that a dog made of bottle caps?"

"Look, Sue, she's made sculptures out of garbage!"

"Do you have classes for adults? I've always wanted to try something like this!"

Tia smiled, fielding the questions with newfound confidence. She explained her philosophy of upcycling, the different techniques she employed, and the various classes she planned to offer. She pointed out examples of her work, from the whimsical cardboard creatures perched on shelves to the intricate mosaics composed of broken glass and ceramics.

"A lot of the techniques I use are the same ones I'll be teaching in my classes, but scaled to the skill level of the participants," she told one father of twin boys. One boy was meticulously coloring in spots on a butterfly he'd added to her garden wall. The other was pretending his stick of chalk was a crushing machine to use on ants.

As the afternoon wore on, the front of the studio became a riot of color. The chalk garden had expanded exponentially, filled with fantastical flowers, bizarre creatures, and heartfelt messages from budding artists. Tia's supply of brochures dwindled until the baskets were completely empty. A happy exhaustion settled over her as the sun began its slow descent.

Finally, as the last strains of music faded from the center of town and the booths began to dismantle, Tia locked up the studio. The exterior was an explosion of color that stretched from the front wall of the studio, spilled onto the sidewalk, and trickled onto the street below. The sight made her happy, but also exhausted at the thought of having to clean it all up. She shrugged. She would face that in the morning.

The bell on the door of the Gingersnap jingled as she entered. Cookie looked up from behind the counter, her face breaking into a wide grin. "Tia, Luv! You look like I feel!"

Tia returned the grin and slid onto one of the stools behind the counter. "Hey, you. Made it through the day in one piece?"

Cookie heaved a sigh, but she was smiling. "Barely. We were swamped! But it was a good swamped, you know? Profitably swamped!" She grabbed two mugs and filled them with steaming coffee, handing one to Tia before tiptoeing over to lock the front door and flipping over the sign on the door. Tia added sugar and cream to her coffee, then followed Cookie to her office.

Both of them kicked off their shoes and propped their feet up on Cookie's desk, letting out matching sighs of contentment.

"So?" Cookie asked, her eyes sparkling with pride. "How'd it go? Tell me everything!"

Tia blew on her coffee before taking a sip. "It was...amazing, actually. Better than I had hoped! I actually ran out of flyers. I've got to get a website up so I can let people know when I schedule classes. I bought the domain name already so I could include it on my cards."

Cookie cheered. "Woo hoo! I knew you would do well!"

Tia laughed. "Let's not get ahead of ourselves. There were also comments about letting me do the pickup of various residents' trash; I could keep what I wanted and bring the rest to the dump. Oh, and of course Sean Reed had to stop by. He looked disappointed at the number of people milling around, and asked if I picked this spot because of how close it was to the fire station." She grimaced, but refused to let his barb sting any longer. Shaking her head, she focused instead on the warm glow the day had given her. "But yeah, it was a good day. A really good day."

A comfortable silence settled over them as they sipped their coffee, both lost in their own thoughts.

Finally, Tia set down her mug and turned to Cookie, a quiet certainty coming to rest in her chest.

"You know, I realize something. Okay, yes, I have to be more careful than I was in high school, but...standing up for my friends, for what's right...The world needs people like that, sometimes."

Cookie smiled, a dimple flashing in her cheek. "Took you long enough, girl! I've been telling you that for years."

Tia grinned. "Yeah, well, sometimes it takes a near-death experience to drive the point home." She paused, then added softly, "I'm proud of myself, Cookie. I'm not running anymore."

Cookie's misty eyes met Tia's gaze. "I'm proud of you, too, Luv. You did good today, and you're going to do even better. This is just the start." She grinned, dispelling the growing sentimentality. Affecting a posh accent, she declared, "Buttonwood Bay is finally going to agree with those of us who already know how great you are!"

Tia wrinkled her nose and stuck her tongue out. She let her head fall back and sighed deeply before dropping her feet from the desk to the floor. "I guess I better head home. I'm glad I've got tomorrow off. I might sleep all day!"

She slipped out the back door to her car in the alley. The pyskies' splash basin was nearly empty, though a large dark circle on the ground around it spoke of the amount of splashing that had occurred throughout the afternoon. She'd have to add water daily, if this kept up.

She approached her car, glancing over behind the flower shop as she unlocked her door. She was sorry that Kiera D'Eath had been murdered, but a soft glow of satisfaction filled her at the thought that she had been able to help bring about justice for her. Now she climbed in and started the car. Her parents and Meela would be eager to hear how well the day had gone, and she couldn't wait to share.

***

Can't get enough of Tia and the cozy fantasy of Buttonwood Bay?

Keep the stories coming! Sign up for my newsletter at piperdow.com and get a free short story explaining just what fire alarm stunt Tia pulled that still has townspeople giving her the side-eye.